THE
WATER
SEER

HMC

The Water Seer

First Edition

ISBN
978-1514864906

ISBN-AUSTRALIA
978-0-646-94479-1

To Pam Daly

whose friendship, inspiration,
and humour I am truly grateful for.

ACKNOWLEDGMENTS

Thank you to my partner in crime, Keith, for watching YouTube videos on how to build stuff so I could spend precious time writing this book.

To the lovely Ana Saiz García for helping me with my Spanish at all hours of the day and night (Google Translate can only do 'so much'). *Gracias¡*

Thank you to David Pacheco for putting your surfing experiences into words for me, and introducing me to the *Soul Surfer*.

Nicky, Yoda, *Sensei*, thank you for being my alpha reader, and taking *The Water Seer* to the next level. Also, to Joe Martin, thank you for taking the time to read my work, and for guiding me to new places. A dad's perspective is always needed!

Once again, to my editor, Carson Buckingham, thank you for your support and genuine care.

Ariel Hudnall, my proofreader, book-formatter, and go-to-lady, you're a superwoman. Are there too many hyphens in this sentence?

Thank you to Kim at KILA Designs. Your book covers are wonderful, and you're such a pleasure to work with – even when I'm a gigantic pain in the butt.

Lastly, a huge thank you to my readers. Your love and support over the past two years, since I first published my work, has given me the inspiration and backbone to continue writing. So, without further ado, please enjoy my third novel, *The Water Seer*.

HMC ♡

Scale of dragon, tooth of wolf,

Witches' mummy, maw and gulf

Of the ravin'd salt-sea shark,

Root of hemlock digg'd i' the dark,

Liver of blaspheming Jew,

Gall of goat, and slips of yew

Silver'd in the moon's eclipse,

Nose of Turk and Tartar's lips,

Finger of birth-strangled babe

Ditch-deliver'd by a drab,

Make the gruel thick and slab:

Add thereto a tiger's chaudron,

For the ingredients of our cauldron.

Double, Double, Toil and Trouble:
Annotations for "The Witches' Chants"
from *Macbeth*, Shakespeare.

CHAPTER 1

SATURDAYS IN BURLEIGH: fresh coffee brewing on James Street, blue skies and golden sand, sand so hot you danced on it, Sadie calling out orders for fish and chips – yes this early in the morning, too – and the sea-salty air obliterating any aggravation from the work week.

Those were my favourite mornings, a time where I could forget death and just surf instead. Surfing was my temporary distraction, a way to calm my mind. It was my creative outlet. An artist painted, a writer wrote, and a surfer surfed. There's the thrill of waiting for the lump, gauging the size and direction of the wave, readying my body – apprehension *and* adrenaline combined – and the wave lifting my feet. I block out the world. It's just me and the wave. The board catches, the world falls away, and I stand. Gravity takes me. The wave knows what to do. It has a mighty energy of its own. For a moment, we dance. I don't thrash and slash the water, I move with it. It's the purest form of surfing, soul surfing, riding the rail with my longboard. It's important to treat the wave with respect.

The other surfers stick their middle finger up if you drop in, but for some reason, I cop it more than most. I don't know if it's because I'm a girl, because I ride a long board, or both. Maybe it's because I surf better than they do. But no one owns the waves. *They* own *you*.

It's not easy to describe the feeling you get after you've just finished an amazing set, unless you're talking to someone with the same passion in spades. I felt that elated, yet peaceful feeling as I made my way home from the beach with my board under one arm, wax sticky and warm from the sun.

I took a left down Elder Entrance. My street was lined with old Queenslanders. Big timber homes, some from the 1800s, built on stumps for windflow. Most of those dinosaurs were fitted with air-conditioners. A few had been torn down and replaced with two-bedroom apartments, but my eyes were always drawn to the old houses.

Mine was the last place on the right, two storeys of cream, maroon, and white, complete with an enormous storage basement. The first storey housed one Toyota and eight years' worth of stuff (including some of my Aunty Catalina's belongings we couldn't get rid of), as well as a giant downstairs laundry and shower – perfect for a surfer with a clean-freak for a mum. Our house might've been old, but it was well-kept.

I unlatched the side gate, entered the laundry, and jumped straight in the shower with my wetsuit to wash the sand and salt water off of me and my surfboard. I dried myself and threw on a sundress.

I skipped every second step to the back door. 'Zat you, Modesta?' Mum, known to others as Ms Castro, or Connie, curled her Spanish tongue around my name. She was the only one who could say it properly. Most people just called me Mouse instead of Modesta. One, because it was easier. Two, because My Aunty's name was Cat. Cat and Mouse – very funny, huh?

Ha de har.

'Good morning.' Mum was in a cheery mood often, despite all she'd been through.

'*Buenos días,*' I said.

'You having a good surf?' Mum grinned, as she chopped tomatoes and threw them into a bowl. She never really had lost her accent. She had come to Australia a little later than Cat.

'Amazing. Thanks. Whatcha makin'?' I pulled myself up on the bench and peered over at the ingredients.

'Modesta, you no sit on this. I cook here. Get down!'

'Mum, please ... I help pay the mortgage. I'll sit where I want.'

'Modesta Castro.' She looked at me like I'd lose a limb if I wasn't careful.

'Okay, okay.' I jumped down off the bench. I put my chin on her shoulder as she chopped. 'Sooo, whatcha makin'?'

She finally laughed. '*Gazpacho*. Hey. Hop offa me. I cannot choop this.'

'Smells so good. Make lots.' I painted on a smile, but underneath I was feeling terrible. The surf had helped eliminate some of the stress I was feeling. It returned, though, like a cork being held under the water. It always bobbed back up again.

'You all right?' Mum sensed my anguish.

'Fine. Just stressed about my internship,' I lied, but only partly.

'You be fine. The little children, they love you.' She smiled.

'Thanks, Mum.' I kissed her on the forehead and made my way to my bedroom.

I opened the door and looked at the papers all over my room. So much work to do. Where to start? I pulled out my laptop and made myself comfortable at my desk. I opened a file named 'lesson plans.' My internship teacher would want to see them on my first day of prac, so I read them over. I was happy to be teaching grade one; I did well with the little ones.

How do we know it's o'clock? What do you do at

7 o'clock in the morning?

I stopped reading.

The tap dripped in my en-suite. Loudly.

Drip. Drip. Drip.

It echoed in my ear.

There was a short, sharp huff on my neck. 'Catalina?' I whispered. 'Are you there?' I waited for a response. 'What is it?' I heard nothing. I closed my eyes. I breathed deeply. I waited for Jon Bon Jovi to sing 'Wanted Dead or Alive' in my ear, to smell the lilac oils Cat wore, or to feel her with me. Hoping, praying it was her come to see me. A visit from my dead Aunt Catalina I could handle; anything else might have tipped me over the edge.

I listened to the water drip.

Agua.

Water brought me closer to the dead – so close, they could tell me their stories, show me their memories, let me see their pain.

There was a sound. I shut my eyes tight. The sound was soft at first. It grew louder. A whistling – a whistling though the teeth to the tune of 'Twinkle Twinkle Little Star.'

Hands reached over the top of mine and lifted me into a standing position. They were smooth. I felt light and warm. I opened my eyes and a woman stood before me. Her brown eyes held my gaze. I saw a tinge of red in them, much like her hair – autumn-coloured and fascinating. She smiled at me. I could smell the salty ocean mist and it soothed me. This woman soothed me. 'Who are you?' I said. No response. 'Where are you? Are you all right?' Still nothing. 'Do you need help? Tell me where you are.' I swallowed. If she didn't give me a clue as to where she was, I wouldn't be able to save her from dying.

My job was to see the future and put a stop to death before it happened, to cheat the Grim Reaper, to save those that *Chalchiuhtlicue* wanted saving. This woman seemed too far gone, like her soul left long ago, and only a whisper of her body remained.

The woman shook her head. She smiled even wider. I looked to her surroundings to try to figure out where she was, but there was only blackness. Her hands suddenly grew cold, but she held on tight ... too tight.

I swallowed.

Her face became grey and translucent, and her hair slick with oil. Scars and sores popped up all over her skin. Her eyes sank into her head, and her teeth transformed into broken and rotten stumps before my eyes. Her tongue slithered out through them. The stench! She squeezed my hands. She was hurting me. 'Let go!' I screamed.

She opened her mouth. Her tongue, gigantic now, flew out and licked my face. It searched for my ear and poked itself inside, searching, searching...

She was inside my head!

Her nails dug into my hands. Her eyes were so red. Her hair was on fire.

Think, Mouse, think.

I closed my eyes. 'Chalchiuhtlicue's light surround. A golden egg. A gate shut tight. With love and light, I protect. Dark witch, *bruja*, I banish you from sight!' I repeated the words over and over, I don't know how many times. Ten? A hundred? Like an auctioneer's litany. A sizzling sound filled the air, followed by a single roll of thunder.

Then, it was over.

I fell down on my bed, breathless. My hands were still bleeding from her nails. I'd never been hurt in *visita* before, and I didn't think it was possible to be injured by a spirit. My heart pounded in rhythm with a killer sudden onset headache. Every minute I'd spent lying awake at night worrying about the visions taking over my life lately, every fear I had been trying to push away in the hopes my problems would disappear like a ghost in a nightmare, were made real by this one experience. Something had come and cut my hands. They stung. And now, not only did I have to worry about zoning out in front of the kids during my internship, I had to worry about having a damned stigmata in front of them, too.

'Mum!' I was finally able to scream. My throat burned. On top of everything else, I was maddeningly thirsty. '¡*Mamá*!'

I felt like I might pass out.

Mum came through my door. 'Modesta.' Her voice never sounded so sweet. She was beside me. 'What happened? A visita? You all right, Modesta!'

I reached up and embraced her. 'No. No, I'm not.'

Mouse's Journal

I was on the Gold Coast Highway, near Sadie's Fish and Chips. A young woman with fluoro-green tights was riding her bike across the intersection, just as a taxi sped through a red light. It hit the bike, swerved, smashed into another vehicle and flipped into the air, killing the bike rider, taxi-driver, and his two passengers. Green Pants got up off the road. Her helmet fell into two pieces, and half her face was missing. She walked over to me. I stuck to the spot, legs like jelly, unable to move. She took off her watch and passed it over. 5:24:35 PM, it said. Although the watch has disappeared with the rest of the vision, I remember every number.

And those pants.

I stood on the corner of Sadie's Fish

and shop for an hour and half that day (not long after the grand-final soccer game I lost because of the visita that made me stand there like a noob). I went early just in case the watch was set to daylight savings or something, and sure enough, a woman on a bike rode along at exactly the right time. It was her. Green Pants. I stepped out in front of her. She tried to swerve. I 'accidentally' fell onto the road and she stopped her bike to help me up. A speeding taxi drove through the red light at the intersection before us; horns blared, cars slammed on their brakes, people shouted profanities out the window and extended middle fingers. There was no collision. No one was hurt.

Green Pants stared at the intersection, then back down at me, a kind of fear and knowing in her grey eyes. Goose bumps rippled up and down my arms.

'Are you okay?' she finally asked.

'I'm so sorry,' I breathed. 'I didn't

even see you.' How could I not see you? I would everyday thereafter, too, you and that green. Green bubble gum tape, GAK, the slime from Ghost Busters, and then those CROCS that Chany - the little Samson girl I used to babysit - wore, would all remind me of you.

I never saw her again, though. Not really. Not after she helped me up, apologised and rode off through the intersection.

CHAPTER 2

I'D ALWAYS THOUGHT of visitas as messages from angels or God intervening, with me as an instrument – like a telephone receiver or something. Well, whatever they are, certain people, apparently important to the master plan up there in some way, are kept alive. A greater good is being fulfilled – at least, I hope so ... I really do.

The tragedy is when you want to see the future, you can't. I later found out that, according to folklore, people with precognitive abilities are unable to tap into their own futures, and that's probably a good thing. When Cat was alive, every now and then, she'd get upset about Nan and Pop – even my dad. Mum had to soothe her. 'I should've seen it coming,' Cat would say. 'What use am I if I can't save the ones I love?' This self-pity never lasted too long. Cat felt deeply, then moved on.

My problem was that I wasn't good at moving on. Now that I had seen this horrible hag-woman's face, I was hard pressed letting it go.

Mum and I were on our way to Anna's. If there was anyone in the world that could help me – contactable in this time-space reality – it was Anna.

The mid-morning traffic wasn't too bad for a Saturday. Mum let me drive her fifteen-year-old, dark brown Toyota to the Esplanade. A few minutes later we were standing before a multi-coloured set of apartment buildings built by an architect trying to think outside the box, with sharp angles and strange shapes. The building looked as if it were straight from the set of a sci-fi flick – an eyesore on such a beautiful beach. But, though it was ugly, I loved it because it was Anna's place. Formerly Anna and Cat's. A safe house, a friend's home, a place filled with memories of my late Aunty. Mum took my arm and we made our way to the intercom. Anna buzzed us up.

When you met Anna out of work, she was relaxed, daggy, and bare-footed. When she spoke about her healing crystals and powders, you expected her to live above some mystical shop, like the occult store in Gremlins, where Randall buys a Mogwai for his son's birthday; the same son who ends up accidently breeding the little monsters that take over the city.

When you met Anna on a workday, she was another person entirely. Anna opened the door in a neatly-pressed pencil skirt and had on a white, long-sleeved shirt. Her platinum-blonde hair was pulled back into a perfect pony tail and she had a lightly made-up face. A school principal often worked weekends. Teachers, too, in fact. Anna had told me all of this before I started uni. 'Are you sure you want to be a teacher, Mouse?' she'd said. 'It's long hours. You'll just get average pay. You really have to love your job.'

I'd smiled at her. 'You know me better than most people, Anna. What do you think?'

She had smiled back. 'I think you'll make a great teacher.'

'Connie, Mouse! It's so good to see you. It's been weeks.' Anna threw her arms around the both of us. She studied me, looked at my bandaged hands, then guided us in. 'Mouse, what happened?'

'I'll tell you all about it. But first, may I please get a glass of water?'

Mum looked at me funny.

'You know where the glasses are. I'll put the kettle on. We'll have chai. Don't worry, I've already been into work. I have the rest of the day for you.'

Anna's apartment was small (and neater than a Myer's store) with her kitchen, lounge, and dining all in one spot – or 'open-planned,' as the real estate agents say. She and Cat had paid it off together pretty quickly, and Anna had tried to give us money for it on several occasions. Mum had said we might take some one day if Anna ever sold it, but probably not. Catalina gave us money when she passed. Mum said it was enough. I'd once asked what Cat had done for a living – I'd never remembered her working. Mum had explained the inheritance from her parents was plenty for both sisters. A great deal of her share had gone into my dad's business and when he died, Mum had sold it for a small fortune.

Carpentry. My dad had been a carpenter. I imagined him with calloused hands, working at a bench, with wood shavings on the ground. He smelled of oil. Whether it was a real memory, I'm not so sure, but I held it dear.

We opened the sliding glass door and made our way out to the balcony. Anna excused herself to get changed while Mum and I took in the view. The sun made the ocean sparkle; the sounds of people calling out to each other and the smell of BBQ put me at ease. I was safe here.

'All right you lovely creatures, what's going on?' Anna brought out the tea. She was in purple shorts and a burnt orange top. She'd put her hair up in a loose bun. This was after-hours Anna. Mogwai Anna. We sipped our tea. It might've been hotter than seven hells out, but we drank tea year round.

'Modesta had the visita,' Mum started.

Anna raised her eye brows. 'How bad?'

'On a scale of one to ten?' I said. 'Off the bloody Richter.'

'Geez, kiddo. Tell me from start to finish.'

I told the story again. Every detail of the woman's face, how it felt, how I used a spell to banish her. I had more questions for Anna than I realised, and they all came pouring out. 'How can I get hurt in a vision? Did that ever happen to Cat?'

'Not that I recall, Mouse.' Anna said.

'Could she have killed me? Why did I have to use a banishing spell in a visita? It's not even real yet … it's supposed to be a future I can change.' I tried to stay calm, but the more I talked about it the more afraid I became. 'I didn't even think I could see my own future, anyway!'

'Calm yourself, now. Your mum and I are here. Cat's here somewhere, too, I'm sure. Nothing's gonna get to you, kiddo. This place has more protection spells around it than Merlin's tower. So does your house.'

'What?' This was news to me. 'Why?'

Mum and Anna glanced at each other, thinking I wouldn't notice.

'Why?'

'Mouse, you have to know,' said Anna, 'that if there are good witches, like you and me, there are bad ones, too.'

Mum put her hand on mine. I knew all about yin and yang. I knew that darkness had to exist for there to be light. But why would this witch be coming for me?

Anna seemed to read my mind.

'I'll get my cards. Let's find out what this bruja wants.' Anna pronounced it 'brewhaa,' just like Cat would've.

Anna left and returned with her deck. They were a

gift from Mum. Anna spread her velvet across the table and wiped her cards with silk. She shuffled the Baraja Española pack. Anna had me touch them and focus on the woman's face. It wasn't hard to do. She hadn't really left my head. That red in her eyes. That awful, snake-like tongue.

A few cards pulled my hand towards them – like they were metal, and my fingers were magnets. I handed them to Anna and she placed them in a gypsy spread from left to right, three rows of seven. One card flew off the table. Mum gasped. Anna picked it up and placed it above the spread. It was an ace – bastos. I knew enough to see the spread was bad. My top card meant lies, bad faith, and death.

Anna surveyed the table. 'Espadas, bastos. This isn't good. There's a woman, jealousy, magic. Fear.' She pointed to the corresponding cards. 'She comes from afar. There is so much pain. And anger. She wants something. Needs it.' Anna spoke fast. 'Here she will find it.' She thought for a second, and shook her head. 'Our homes become unstable, I'm afraid. Fear escalates and spreads. We must protect ourselves. We must protect…' Anna put a hand over a card. She pulled away suddenly. Anna stared at me and swallowed. 'She comes.'

This was like a bad horror movie.

'Who come?' Mum put a hand over her mouth. 'Now?'

'Anna?' I said. She was far away. Her eyes lost their usual glimmer. Anna's face was drawn. I reached over and grabbed her shoulder. 'Anna!' I shook her.

Anna's mouth opened wide. Her voice was high-pitched, like a child's. 'Saaaacmiiiiiiiiisssssssssssss.' She continued to hiss, until I stood and pulled her up out of her chair. 'Anna.'

Mum ran from the balcony and returned with the pitcher of cold water. 'Wake up. You wake up NOW.' She threw the cold water over Anna.

Anna coughed and spluttered. She inhaled to catch her breath. 'Cold! Cold! Cold!' she said.

Mum and I held onto her until she calmed. 'You're okay,' I said. 'You're okay now.'

After a few moments, Anna was able to sit down. I fetched a towel from inside and draped it over her shoulders. Anna shuddered. 'What was that?' I've never had anything like that happen to me before. I left my body, but I heard what I was saying. I kind of said it, but I didn't ... Sacmis?' Anna looked at me.

I nodded. 'Sacmis.'

I was seven or eight when Cat first told me the story. It was one of many. I pictured Cat's face now, her dark hair hanging around her shoulders and her Spanish eyes fixed upon mine. 'I have this story in my journal.' I pulled the thick, tattered book out of my bag. I turned to the front, where I had written several stories down.

Sacmis was a little girl, found by the villagers next to the River Nile, close to the ancient Egyptian

city of Luxor. She was found with nothing but the clothes on her back. Her body was black and blue with bruises, and red with wounds. From what or who, no one knew. She was alone.

She said nothing but her own name. No one knew where she came from, or what terrors she'd seen. Some said she sprung from the River Nile itself, and the trip left her battered and broken. Some say the Gods were punishing her and she was left to live as a human – to endure the suffering of this world.

Her hair was copper, and her eyes shone with a red in the sun never seen before by the people. She was beautiful. But, beauty meant nothing when food was scarce. No one could take Sacmis in.

Though his family was scraping by, a farmer named Ptah took Sacmis into his home. Ptah and his wife were kind and loving, and they gave Sacmis everything they could. But soon, his own two children – a son and a daughter – grew jealous of Sacmis. They teased her and called her names.

The more the children taunted Sacmis, the better Ptah and his wife treated her to make up for their childrens' foibles. Still Sacmis did not speak, which only gave the children encouragement to continue their bullying.

Ptah struggled to keep his family fed. Before too long, bread, salted fish, and geese appeared in the farm house. Ptah knew it was Sacmis. How she came by these goods he didn't know. Thankful to the Gods for his luck, Ptah fed and cared for Sacmis and his family until she came of age. Rather than leave home, she stayed on, helping with the cooking and mending. Ptah's children grew up and moved on, but they never accepted Sacmis. Eventually, they had children of their own.

One day, Ptah's boss knocked on his door, and told Ptah he'd be receiving a raise. This was unheard of in the village, and news spread of Ptah's good fortune. His wife was thrilled, and tried to persuade him it was due to his excellent work.

The villagers soon forgot the suffering Ptah and his family had been through in the past. They only resented his special treatment.

Though Ptah knew they were jealous of his good fortune, the villagers gave him the best cuts of meat, the freshest grapes and figs, and even invited him to their homes. He turned them down. Ptah knew when they were being overly kind, it was Sacmis. Somehow, it was her influence that had brought it about. Was it some kind of magic? Ptah didn't know, but one thing was certain – magic was trouble, and the attention from the villagers was becoming too much for a quiet man.

Sacmis returned one day and Ptah noticed her belly was growing round. He thought it could be from the extra food, but as time went on, Sacmis continued to grow. He wondered which man in the village had done this to her. Because of her beauty, there were many young men who fussed over her. How could he tell which?

'Sacmis, name the father of the child you carry,' he whispered one day, as they stood together outside, by the river. She shook her head. 'Tell me,' Ptah said. Still, Sacmis shook her head. She sighed heavily, and threw her arms around Ptah. She sobbed. He stroked her hair. 'What will become of this?' he said to the wind.

That night, Ptah spoke to his wife. 'That girl is with child,' he said. 'We already have enough trouble with the people of the village. It's time she left.' Ptah had made up his mind, and there was nothing his wife could do to stop him. Upon their visit with the grandchildren, Ptahs' son and daughter were happy to hear the news. 'We've never liked her. She causes nothing but trouble,' said the daughter. And the more they talked, the worse their revisionist history regarding the poor girl became, and even the wife joined in. It made them feel justified in casting her aside. Ptah's ending words were, 'She's brought shame upon our family, and must leave at once.'

Little did they know, Sacmis had heard the conversation. She sat by the side of the house and wept with her hand on her stomach. The ache in her heart was so overwhelming she could hardly breathe. That night, as she walked on, with no place to go to, there was a sharp pain in her stomach. Soon blood trickled down her leg.

Sacmis lost the babe – the only human that might have ever truly loved her.

It was in that moment, weeping on the ground, with blood beneath her, and with all that she'd lost screaming in her head, that Sacmis forgot everything human within her heart.

And that night, something evil possessed Ptah. He killed everyone in the village with his bare hands, including his very own wife, children, and grandchildren.

I placed my journal down. Mum held a hand on her heart.

Anna studied me. She sipped her tea. The laughter of the kids across the road playing football in the sunshine seemed out of place, and it felt as though it should've been night time, with a howling wind whipping up the ocean to set the mood. Instead, people were strolling, exercising, and having a big day out with their children. Meanwhile, I was I wondering how safe my tiny family and I were from some evil force that might be inclined to visit at any given moment. *Peekaboo ... I see you.*

'I don't think you had a visita, Mouse,' Anna said. 'I know it's not a spirit. Cat would never have allowed that. As you mentioned, it came through when you listened to the water in your sink. Your agua. Now, if there'd been a roaring fire in your bathroom, I'd have doubts. Then there's the protection spells around your house...' Anna was thinking.

'Could it be some kind of message from another source? A warning maybe?' I said.

She nodded. 'It makes sense.'

I thought for a moment. 'But why couldn't Cat, or the guide – or whoever – just come instead of showing me that horrid woman? Plus, it hurt me.'

Anna shook her head. 'Good question. Maybe whoever it was isn't trained in the craft. Perhaps showing you the threat was more effective.'

'Right. Thanks, newbie, for scaring the beejeesus out of me and ripping up my hand. I wish Cat was here.' The words escaped before I could suck them back in.

Mum rubbed my shoulder. 'Catalina will come.' I put my hand over hers. Mum's warm skin, and the sparkle in her eyes, reminded me I wasn't alone. It was lucky for me I had these two special women in my life and they had some idea what was going on. I hadn't meant to sound ungrateful – I was lucky to have them. Experiencing this on my own would've been frightening. Well, even more so.

I sipped my tea. The taste and scent of the chai was a comfort. 'What do you think this woman wants?' I asked Anna.

She licked her lips and studied the cards. After a while, she looked up at us. 'Honestly?' She pointed to the two bastos. 'A child,' she said. 'I think this thing wants a child.'

Mum gasped. She put a hand up to her mouth, as if to cover up a scream.

'Well she can't have any of my children.' Anna folded her arms, referring to the 542 students in her care. 'No way, no how.'

'What are we going to do about it?' I said.

Anna looked at Mum. 'What do you think, Connie? Do we wait this out a little?'

Mum thought for a moment. She glanced at the kids playing football across the road and kept her eyes on them as she spoke. 'We wait.' She turned back to me. 'Modesta, you must watch for the signs. Whatever is coming, we need more to know.'

'Agreed,' said Anna. She ran a hand over her spread, as if the cards might change. 'How this woman is related to Sacmis, I don't know. I can't mine much more from this reading, but I'm sure it will come to us.'

I exhaled. It wasn't until I loosened my neck and shoulders that I realised how tense I was. 'I have to remember that trick,' I said.

'Which trick is that?' said Anna.

'The one where you relax and let the Universe tell you all you need to know – especially under circumstances like these. It's impossible.'

Anna nodded. 'Don't worry. Somehow, I have a feeling we won't have to wait long.' She finished her tea. 'Mouse?'

'Yeah?'

'Stay away from your bathroom,' she said.

I laughed, even though I could've cried instead. 'Not a prob, Anna.'

Mouse's Journal

My first visita. Noon (I think) April, 2006. Elder Entrance house, backyard.

Roman is a golden retriever. He is a shiny-coated puppy with eyes that never leave me. I was swinging on my tire in the backyard - it's still connected to the sugar gum - when I first saw him. I was missing Cat that day because I was wishing she could see the new house. I was thinking how lonely it would be on Anna's balcony with just the three of us. I was angry because I thought I'd never learn to be a water seer like Cat now she was gone. Anna was special, but she wasn't my Aunty.

Mum was cooking in the kitchen. I could hear her banging pots and pans around to soothe her aching heart. Cooking did that for her. Not me, though. I needed the ocean, the trees, or at least the sky above.

Back and forth I went, swinging, hoping to hear her again. 'I miss you, Cat,' I whispered to no one. The smell of lilac hit me. I could almost feel the oil on my skin. The distant sound of Bon Jovi crooned about how he was a cowboy, and on a steel horse he'd ride.

'You'll be all right, Sirenita,' she replied.

'Cat?'

'This is Roman,' she said. The golden puppy appeared before me.

'Whoa! He's so cute!' I jumped off the swing and bent down to pat Roman. My hand went straight through him. I gasped and fell to my knees. Roman disappeared.

'Cat? What happened?'

'Roman needs your help, Mouse. He's lost. He'll be passing by your house in about five minutes, and I want you to go out the front, pick him up, and bring him upstairs. He's a good boy. He'll let you carry him. He needs to go home.

Can you do that, Sirenita?'

'Yes, Aunty.' I was hesitant. As you can imagine, Cat sounded in my head like my own thoughts. I could've been talking to myself ... and answering. Even scarier.

I sat on the short brick wall that was - and still is - my front fence. After the fourth minute, I felt as if I'd definitely imagined the whole thing. I was so young, confused and terrified I'd started hearing voices. I'd be passenger one on the next bus to crazy town. Population: tea.

Sure enough, Roman plodded down the path, cute as he was in my vision, but this time real.

'Come here, Roman! Good boy. Oh, you're a good boy.' I picked him up and took him upstairs to Mum.

'What you have there, Modesta? He is a pretty boy, he is.' Mum patted Roman on the head, and then frowned. 'You cannot be taking people's dogs. Where he come from? You take him back.'

'He needs to go home. Can we call the number? It's written on his dog collar,' I pleaded.

'Very good.' Mum called and Roman was picked up within the hour.

I went to see Roman a few times after that. He's now around two-and-a-half years away from retiring as a guide dog for a man called Rodney Spencer.

'Good job, Sirenita,' Cat said, as I lay on my bed, waiting for dinner that night. I held a photo of her as she spoke, and pretended it was a normal conversation with two living people. Not weird at all.

'Will you come back again?' I said.

Cat sighed. 'Yes.'

'When?'

'I don't know, my sweet. But one thing you must know is, you're a water seer now, just like you wanted. There will be things you have to do, and you're going to have to be brave, you hear?'

'What kinds of things, Aunty?' I sniffed.

'Listening to agua. Looking for signs. Learning your craft. Anna will teach you. Your mother will be your anchor. Do you know what that means?' I did. I nodded. 'You have to listen, and you have to obey. There are consequences if you don't.'

'You mean punishment if I don't do the job?' I said.

'Sort of. You'll do just fine, though. But if you ignore the messages, if you ignore the warnings, bad luck follows. You understand? I know from experience.'

I rolled over on my bed and stared at her photo. 'I'm scared.'

'I know, Sirenita. We had no choice. You are the only female left in our family with a strong connection to agua. It won't be easy, but I'll be around to help. Okay? I love you.'

'I love you, Aunty.'

CHAPTER 3

'YOU ALL RIGHT, MATE?' A scruffy man glared over the counter. His face was familiar. He was one of the recovering addicts who used the methadone clinic across the street, and came in for a sandwich and cream bun most days.

'Sorry. Yeah, I'm okay.' I was at work at the bakery. *Focus, Mouse.*

I tried to gain balance over my body. He passed me a ten dollar note and waited, but I didn't know what to punch into the till. I looked at the counter and saw a sandwich bag and a cream bun. *Okay, think, girlie. Concentrate.* '$6.40 for one sandwich and a cream bun.' I waited another second in case he corrected me and rang it up. '$3.60 change. Have a good day.'

'See ya.' He left with his food, and I took several deep, controlled breaths to steady myself. My thoughts were bouncing around my head like an echo in a cave. I swayed a little. For a moment, I'd forgotten where I was and what I was doing. It was like I'd just woken up in the bakery and had to retrace my steps. How I'd come to be at work all flooded back, but not like reaching for a normal memory – more like reaching for one from a week or two ago.

The morning's little event popped into my head like a nightmare from childhood. *Sacmis.* Anna and Mum would still be drinking tea and talking about it, including whatever it is they were hiding from me. They way they'd stolen glances at each other as if I wouldn't notice. Was I being paranoid? *Maybe.*

I heard whistling from the back of the shop. It was Reggie making pies. The smell of pastry wafted through the bakery. The Ashes were playing on the ABC Grandstand radio, and I could just make out what the commentators were saying. Australia was winning. Reggie had recorded it and had played it a few times this month. Australia hadn't won in years, and Reggie's mind was still fresh with our success in the nineties – over a decade without a loss. 'Them's were the days we always beat those poms. Cricket's changed,' he'd say. 'The world's changed, Mouse. You never got somethin' for nothin' back when I was growin' up. Ya did the hard yards, and you might get what ya wanted if you were lucky, might not. 'Pends on which way the wind blew, mate.'

I took a sip of water and watched as a mum pushed her stroller past the bakery window.

Bastos. The child.

Anna had put a protection spell on us all, but we couldn't possibly do that for every child. No witch's circle of protection stretched that far. If this thousands-of-years-old-Sacmis-woman showed up, I'm not sure how well our spells would work, anyway. *Begone! Or I'll smite thee with my sage!* Oh dear, if Cat could hear me now, I'd cop a wallop across the back of the head. 'Sorry, Cat. No disrespect.'

'Huh?' My boss, Reggie, called from the kitchen.

'Nothin', Reg,' I called back.

For now, I wanted to go on as normal.

'Mouse, give us a hand, will ya?' Reggie called.

'Coming.' The oven heated the already oppressive room, but there was no air conditioner – not in this old school, run-down place. Besides, the front had no walls, just a pull-down garage door. Even if we got an air-con, the sweet, cool air would just dance on out into the flaming atmosphere that was summer on the Gold Coast.

Reggie stood over a tray of curried-chicken pies, placing a leaf-shaped pastry on top to identify them later. The BEST PIES ON THE GOLD COAST sign out front meant a lot to him. The money went into the quality food, not the decorating.

I glanced at the calendar. I still needed to document my visita from this morning. In all the craziness, I'd forgotten. 'What's the date again, Reg?'

'Ahhh, the 25th. How could you forget? Tomorrow's Australia Day.' He didn't look up from his work. I jotted the date down on a sticky note, along with the approximate time the bruja showed up this morning. I shoved the note in my pocket so I could write it all down in my journal later on.

'Survival Day, you mean?' I said. 'Invasion Day? Day where England stole...'

'I know, I know. I acknowledge the traditional owners of this here great land, Mouse, just as much as the next fella. Just like yourself.'

'I'm just stirring you, Reg. I know you do. But we really should move the date.'

'Maybe we can have our party a weekend early. Start some kinda Aussie Day trend. Move the *Triple J* countdown. Anyway, sorry you can't make it this year,' he said.

'Me, too. I have my first day of school on Tuesday, teaching grade one. I have to be ready,' I said, remembering out loud. How could I plan lessons and teach in the state I was in? At least I had Monday off. Even though Sunday was Australia Day, we still got our public holiday.

'That's all right. We'll have a beer for you. Or seven.' Reggie let Trent and I have a few at his BBQs. We weren't far off legal age, but Mum would still freak out. She was firm on the alcohol rule.

I looked up at the round school clock on the wall, and noticed it was three o'clock. The afternoon had flown by.

'Are you okay? You've been a bit distant today. Somethin' on yer mind?' said Reggie.

Ha! You don't wanna know. I shook my head. 'Just thinking about school, is all. Sorry. I'll try to stay focussed.' He still looked worried. It was hard to put anything past Reggie. He was a beer-drinking, sport-loving Aussie, but Reginald Spence was in touch with his feelings.

'University is hard work,' I went on. Maybe that's all it was, a little mental breakdown. But that didn't explain Anna's reading, and whatever had happened to *her* that morning. Or the cuts on my hands. I'd had to tell Reggie it was the rocks at Burleigh. He was mad I'd surfed near the headland.

'Well as long as you're okay. Can you watch the mince, please?' he said.

'Sure.' I took a deep breath and added Italian herbs to the pot of bubbling meat, busying myself with the next day's pastries. They weren't for the shop. They were for Reg's *Triple J* Top 40 countdown extravaganza by the pool. His pool was fit with a slippery dip, and beside it, Reggie had built a Bali-hut with a dining table to fit nine, a mini bar, and fridge for the beer. He'd worked hard to earn enough to buy a house for his family. He'd done a killer job on his yard over the past decade. Pity his ex-wife had never appreciated it.

The buzzer jolted me back to reality – a customer. I washed my hands and dried them on my apron.

'Coming! What can I get…' I stepped through the doorway and halted. It was Trent. 'Think of the devil, and that S.O.B. will show right up on your doorstep lookin' for a sausage roll,' I said.

He smiled at me with his lop-sided, cabbage-patch dimples. His skateboard was in his hand. 'Awww, you were thinkin' about me? I'm spesh. How are ya, Mousie?' Trent Albright was a sight for sore eyes. He frowned at me. 'What happened to your hand?'

I looked down at the bandages. I felt like Mum had gone overboard now, wrapping them up like that. 'Oh, just the rocks.' I felt bad lying to my best mate, but he'd live.

'How was the surf this morning? Apart from slashing your hands up?' Bruno, Trent's staffy, was by the door, tied to a pole and almost choking himself to get in the shop. 'Sit, Bruno!' he shouted. The dog tried to run at him and got coat-hangered in the process.

'Small, but good.'

'You up for tomorrow?' he asked.

'For sure. Five?'

'Yep. Sounds good.' Trent and I often surfed on Sunday mornings, especially during summer. We wanted to go super early, before the Australia Day crowds.

'So, I'll have a chicken, mayo, lettuce, and tomato on white-and-sliced thick, please,' he said.

I laughed. 'Sure.' I turned toward the bar and sliced the loaf. As I was slicing, I remembered Anna had put me into Sonny's grade one class for my internship. He was Trent's little brother. 'Is Sonny happy I'm going to be teaching in his classroom?'

'Are you kidding me? He flipped his lid! He wants to know if he can still call you Mouse, or if it has to be Miss Castro. I told him to call you Miss Mouse. It has a nice ring.'

'Great, that's gonna stick.' I shook my head.

'I'm hoping so. Hey, don't be stingy with the chicken, either.'

'Shush your bush!' I said. 'I could lather Sonny like butter on toast for breakfast every day of the week, by the way.'

'Yeah, he feels the same about you.'

Sonny wasn't just a sweet little blondie who could tear it up on a short-board, he was smart, too. Because his parents had been trying to have him since Trent was born, Trent had been waiting for a little brother or sister most of his life. Trent and I had been sitting in his room watching Stephen King's *IT* on his laptop, with the sound turned down so we wouldn't get caught, when his Mum broke the news she was pregnant. I'll never forget that moment, or the movie – Pennywise the clown kept me away from circuses forever.

I remember the day Sonny was born. He'd looked like a squished-up, little old man with a misshapen head. That head turned out to be a pretty damned cute one – butter-wouldn't-melt cute.

'Here's hoping his whole class is as well-behaved as he is. My last prac nearly killed me.' I wrapped Trent's sandwich.

'I remember that. Prep, right? Those five-year-olds! Watch out, they'll cut ya if you're not careful.'

'Seriously, if you taught that class for one day, you'd have had a mental breakdown. Imagine Sonny jacked up on red cordial and then times him by thirty,' I said.

'I've never said I could teach. In fact, I think you're insane. My prac is already shaping up to be awesome, as well. The legal secretary there has a mouth the size of her entire head, and the coffee tastes like arse. And not the good kind.'

'There's a good kind?' I laughed. 'Gross.'

'Hey, Albright, stop distracting my staff!' Reggie said as he came out from the back.

'Hey, Reggie.' Trent said.

'You gonna pay for that?' he said, pointing at Trent's sandwich.

'Probably not.' Trent shook his head with a wide grin.

'You're a bloody pain in my nether-regions, Albright. Tell your Dad your tab's now twenty-one bucks, and fifty-cents for interest.'

'Your nether-regions? Which area exactly *in* your nether-regions?' Trent smirked.

'Getta outta here, ya tight-arse.' Reggie threw his hands up.

'I'm going, I'm going. And by the way, there's a new bakery opening up in Miami, and the papers are talking about how they have the best pies on the

Gold Coast. Just sayin'.'

Reggie picked up a multigrain bread roll and threw it at Trent. 'Out!' They both laughed and Trent disentangled Bruno from the pole outside.

'Tomorrow, Mouse!' Trent called.

'See ya, mate.' I waved them off as Bruno pulled Trent along on his skateboard, and Trent ate his free chicken and mayo sandwich with the other hand. They were both almost falling into the highway traffic. I shook my head. That guy attracted danger and never got hurt. Trent Albright was kissed on the butt by fairies.

'Good kid, that one,' said Reggie. 'Why you two never hooked up, I'll never know.'

Reggie wouldn't find out for a long time, too. Trent just wasn't ready. I'll never forget the time I'd tried to kiss him a few years back. He froze like a deer in headlights then took off, terrified, on his skateboard. That afternoon he hand-delivered *the letter*.

Dear Mouse,

I love you. I love you so much I want to stab myself in the eyes with a burning iron rod. I know that's not very romantic, but that's how I feel. You're the best friend I've ever had. You're the only friend, actually, which is perfect in my opinion, because you're perfect.

Perfect in every way.

But I'm so sorry. I'm so sorry about today when you tried to kiss me. If only I was different. If I was different, I would have kissed you back. If I was different, we'd get married and have a thousand babies, because I love you!

You see, Mousey, no one knows this, but I'm not attracted to girls. Yup. Me. Trent. Don't like girls that way. Wish I did. But I don't.

I haven't told anyone yet, because I'm pretty scared, as you can imagine. I'm not the kind of gay guy who everyone suspected as a kid. The one who grows up and says, 'Hey, I'm gay!' and everyone is like: 'Ah, yeah … we know, dickhead.'

I'm the skater with a staffie and a foul mouth. No one suspects me. I wasn't even certain myself until recently.

You deserve to be with the most amazing person in the cosmos. It just can't be me.

Don't worry, I'll make sure you don't date any losers, and if anyone hurts you, I'll poke THEIR eyes out with said burning iron rod. K?

Hope you're all right.

Hope WE'RE all right.

Your bestie, forever.

Trent.

It hurt like one-hundred simultaneous needles, at first. It was a sting I'll never forget. Well, more like a throb – a throbbing ache in my hollow heart. The boy I'd fallen in love with would never be mine.

'Go get that bread roll will ya, Mouse? Put it in the bin before we attract the Ibis.' I grinned as Reggie turned and got back to his pies. I couldn't dispose of the multigrain roll that was meant to hit Trent in the head. It had been annihilated by the highway cars.

I finished the pies and realised I'd been daydreaming. Reggie was packing bags of bread for the end of the day. He passed me two large bags filled with loaves and buns, and kept two for old Keith, who picked them up on a Saturday afternoon to take back to his over-sized family on Mount Tamborine. 'Thanks.' I took them and swung the bread over my shoulder. 'See you Wednesday, Reggie. Remember, it's my first week of prac, so I'll be in just on time each day.'

'Night, Mouse. Thanks for today. And good luck on your first day at school, teach. You'll smash it. Happy Australia Day. Won't be the same without you two tomorrow.'

'Thanks. Have a good one.'

The sun was so bright drivers on the highway shielded their eyes, despite already being protected by sunglasses and tinted windows. Nothing like the smell of burnt rubber and exhaust fumes in the afternoon.

As I crossed the highway, I still felt like a bag of nerves. Although I was surrounded with Anna's white magic, I felt vulnerable. I was a rookie with protection spells. My visitas and good timing were all I'd ever needed in the past. Anna was hell-bent on setting that straight as soon as possible, and I was good with it. She'd be home when I got there tonight. I didn't want to be a wuss, living in fear, but I wasn't stupid. Something was coming. We needed to prepare. *Gloves off, baby.*

A bald tweeker leaned against the health-clinic wall. She had a tattoo across her neck, skeletal wings spanned from ear to ear. It wasn't top-notch, but mid-range at least. I wondered how she'd gotten the money for it. Some tattooists on the Gold Coast were around 150 an hour. This looked like a whole-day sitting. 'Got a spare ciggi?' she asked.

'Nah, sorry. I don't smoke.' I kept walking. Just then, Santa Claus turned the corner and came my way. Not the real Saint Nick, or even a man dressed in the suit made famous by *Coca-Cola*. This Santa wore a white singlet and pushed a trolley full of old goods – spare bike parts, a cask of goon, blankets, and today, he had a DVD player and a carton of cigarettes. His long white beard and prominent beer-belly made children run toward him, and parents pull them back in horror. Santa passed by, stopped at the tweeker, pulled out a cigarette from his carton, and gave it to her with a grin. Rumour was he didn't even smoke. Other rumours suggested he was more like Robin Hood in that he stole from the rich and gave to the poor.

Trent said that wasn't true. 'Dad says Santa comes in for a cuppa at Abby's now and then. One day they chatted and Dad found out Ray – Ray's his actual name – spends his *Centrelink* money on things he can fix and sell, or give away. Ray even works for the dole doing paintings on the highway. You know the beautification project? Did you know they help paint those?' he'd asked.

I did know it. Mum had done some work for the dole when she was between jobs. She'd painted a *Harry Potter* banner for the local library. It was amazing. I'd asked her to do one for my classroom when I became a teacher. It sat rolled up in my cupboard awaiting its debut. I left Santa and Tweeker to their business.

Abby's Vans was run by Rick Albright and his family out of a building to the back of the clinic. I entered. 'Mouse!' Sonny Albright ran up and hugged me tight.

'Hey, what are you doing here, little tiger?' He often spent Saturdays with his nanna. 'Still not too old for hugs. Argh! Careful, you're stronger than you think.' He grinned at up at me with little boy missing teeth, and held up a Superman figurine. I couldn't tell if it was new or old, as they'd remade the movie not too long ago. 'Cool.'

'You're gonna be in my claaaaaaaass.' His enthusiasm was infectious.

'Yes I am. You better be on your best behaviour!'

'Will you teach us instead of Mrs Lawson?' he asked.

'Some days.'

'Cool!' Sonny lifted his action figure and drove it toward me in slow motion. 'Brrrrrrjjjjjjjj. The Evil Mouse Giant ducks for cover but Superman smashes her in the face.' Sonny waits. 'Mouse, you have to duck!' I complied as Superman crashed into me and I pretended to tumble back to the ground.

'Argh! You've killed me, you vile crusader for justice! I'll be back, Superman.' I closed my eyes, chocked, gurgled and 'died.'

Sonny spoke in a deep voice. 'The Evil Mouse splutters and coughs up blood from her foaming mouth. But what Superman doesn't know is that she's really just sleeping, lying down with her eyes closed and waiting to gather strength and kill again.'

'Hi, Mouse. How are you, mate?' Rick Albright held out a strong hand and helped me up, then grabbed the bread bags and put them up on the counter. 'Sonny, have you been slaying dragons again?'

'No! Giant mice.'

'Well, Superman, your mum wants a word.' Rick chuckled.

'Uh oh, you're in trouble.' I slugged him on the shoulder.

'See ya!' Sonny pelted past.

'And where did you get that toy, anyway?' Rick called. Sonny was gone before he could answer. 'Where he gets this stuff, I don't know.' He shook his head.

I was left standing there staring at an older version

of my best friend, Trent. Rick Albright made the stone-in-my-gut feeling wash away pretty quickly. He had that way about him – Father of the Year.

'Trent wanted me to remind you of your surf tomorrow. Better get down there before the Australia Day crowds,' he said.

'Yep. I won't forget. We're meeting at five, so we should be right.'

'How's your mum?' he asked.

'She's good.'

'Carey wants you both over for a roast ASAP. All right? Give her a call tomorrow if you can.' Rick was gathering paper cups and plates for this evening's run. He'd be out most of the night serving the homeless. Abby's was a mobile soup kitchen. Abby, the matriarch of the Albright family, had been picked up and dusted off by a volunteer from a soup kitchen when she had lost her job, and had to raise two sons on her own, as well. Not only did she end up raising two gentlemen, one of which went on to have my awesome bestie, Trent, but she sponsored those who served the homeless with every extra bit of cash she had. She had eventually gotten her very own van and joined the cause.

'Shall I wait until after the long weekend to call?' I said, raising my eyebrows.

'Mouse, my wife would answer her phone for you if the house was on fire.'

Carey was a wonderful mother, and now that I was older, I considered her a friend. I grinned at

Rick. 'I'll call her.'

He gave me a knowing nod. 'Thanks for the bread. Tell Reggie I said thanks again, too. He's an absolute legend.'

'No worries. See you Wednesday, Rick.'

'Or before, if Carey has a say.' He waved me off.

Mouse's Journal

My third visita - 2nd April, 2008 at 9A.M.
Trent's backyard, Burleigh Waters
House.

 An elderly woman walked up to me as
I stood in Trent's backyard. She took
my hand and walked me into a hall
that appeared.

 Fifty old people crammed into a hall.
The air-conditioning was on during
a particularly hot autumn day. A
gentlemen with a large moustache
called out numbers at the front of the
hall, and a bird-nosed woman looked over
the scorecards of the fellow bingoers to
make sure all was in order. He spidery
fingers pulled strands of fine hair from
her face.

 I was scared. It was my first
visita away from home - one where I
was taken from the familiar and shoved
into a foreign, future, dangerous place.

I expected a puppy, like Roman. This wasn't that kind of visita.

There was a creaking sound as the hall seemed to shift. The people in the room stopped and gasped, assessed the noise, decided it was nothing and went on playing. I knew it was far from nothing. My heart thumped.

The next thing I knew, there were beams falling from the ceiling. There was shrieking and panic. Dust flew and people scattered. They weren't fast enough. Darkness fell upon me.

The next moment I was outside, looking at the wreckage of the hall.

There were no survivors.

The 'Gold Coast Aged Care' bus sat like a sleeping mastodon in the car park as if nothing had happened. Like it was waiting to take everyone home. When night fell, Trent and I snuck out and slashed the tires of the bus. The hall collapsed the next day, but there was no one inside it.

CHAPTER 4

BERGAMOT BURNED BESIDE US. Rain was hitting the windows as the nightly summer storm cooled the house. Mum and Anna held my hands as we sat at our dining table. Anna chanted. Whispers entered my head as if there were a few more people besides Anna chanting. I opened my eyes to check, but there were no extra bodies. The candles flickered, lighting the dim room, and I wondered, guiltily, how something like this could really protect us from a bruja like the one I saw in my vision this morning. Just us three sitting at our dining table with some incense, thinking that it was going to do anything … *Woo, aren't we scary.*

Anna opened her eyes and looked at me.

'Concentrate, Mouse. This isn't going to work without you.' I let my shoulders relax, closed my eyes, and focussed. She was right. What was with me lately? I loved the craft. Anna had a sixth-sense for non-believers and right now I was flailing. 'Protect us with all your might, oh Goddess gracious day and night,' Anna said.

Mum and I chanted with her. I felt myself loosen. I moved into the chant. A warm, soft feeling enveloped my body. *This* was what I loved. Magic wrapped up my soul. My mind wandered to a higher place. My arms and legs felt triple their size, and so heavy I couldn't shift them. I didn't want to. The meditative state I was in was the best I'd felt in weeks. I stopped chanting. It was too much work to move my mouth now. I let my breath be the centre, my body an instrument of magic, with white light pouring through to my bones and back again, and I imagined an egg surrounding us. It hardened. We were shielded. Purple for sleep, green for healing, and white for protection.

After a while Anna spoke, 'We're done.' She smiled at us. 'Good job, Mouse. You really helped the process.'

Mum studied me. 'You okay, Modesta? You look tired now.'

I nodded. 'I am a little. In a good way, though.' I yawned.

'You want tea?'

'Yeah. Thanks,' I said. Mum stood and went to the kitchen.

'I meant it. You did really well, kiddo. *When* you

focussed.' Anna squeezed my hand.

'Do you think this will be enough?' I asked.

Anna nodded. 'For now.'

'I was thinking we could do a séance, or something. Talk to Cat properly, you know? She knows what's going on, I'm sure, but I've heard nothing from her.' I said.

'You know that's a terrible idea. Every horror story with a Ouija board is partly true, Modesta. And you remember that poltergeist we conjured.'

I did remember. How could I forget? Anna and Cat had once tried to contact Dad so Mum could speak to him. Something went wrong, as they sometimes do when messing with the other side, and we had a poltergeist on our hands for several days. I was eight. It had been terrifying, because poltergeist love children and teens, so I was the one it attached itself to. Luckily for me, all it had done was flush the toilet at random intervals, make the house smell like burnt toffee, and change the notes in my diary to gibberish. The worst part was when it breathed in my ear one night, but by that point I had Anna, Cat, and Mum all sleeping in the same room with me, so as soon as I had screamed, the thing took off faster than Cathy Freeman at the starter pistol.

'I know,' I said. 'It's just ... what about the kid?' I finally asked the question that had been on my mind all day. '*Bastos.*'

'I've been thinking about that.' Anna was packing her bergamot and candles into a velvet-lined bag where she stored all her magic paraphernalia. 'I think if we're entwined – which is likely – we'll find out all we need to know.'

'Right.' I wasn't totally convinced. I was never good at waiting. The kettle boiled in the kitchen and I could hear Mum shuffling about.

Anna reached into her bag. 'Don't worry, I wouldn't just leave it to fate.' Anna swapped her incense and candles for a small, shear-white bag. She passed it to me and I smelled it.

'Mugwort, cinnamon.' I took another smell and fingered the bag. 'Star anise,' I said. 'Mugwort for divination and dreaming.' I thought back to my lessons with Anna. 'Cinnamon for protection. Star anise for contacting other planes.'

'Very good!'

Mum shuffled in with a tray of tea. It smelled delicious. 'What you do with those things?' she said.

'She'll put them in water,' said Anna. 'A bath should do the trick, Mouse.' She looked at me. I nodded. At least she didn't want me to have a shower in that bloody-awful en-suite.

'She will see Catalina with these things?' Mum asked.

Anna nodded. 'That's the plan.'

'Why can't I hear her right now?' I said. 'I mean, I could never really summon her up to speak, but she's always come to me in times of need. Just … naturally.' I studied Anna as she thought.

'I don't know. It's strange. And I don't like it. Not

any of it. This is why we have to go to her, and I'm sorry, Mouse, but you're the best medium between us. It has to be you.'

Mum took the bag from the table and sniffed them. 'I never was interesting in the herb magic. I like the magic where you say the spells aloud. Like the chanting we do. I feel like they really work. Catalina, she was so very good at the chanting spells.' Mum smiled, and placed the bag down before me. She poured us tea and sat to sip her own. We waited for her to go on. She didn't disappoint. 'Catalina once made a boy fall in love with me.' Mum chuckled. 'He was so very handsome with big brown eyes. You should've seen his eyelashes. Sabatino was his name. I was thirteen years old. At first, of course, he did not seeing me at all. Then, all of sudden, he was the love-struck! I knew it was Catalina because she told me years later.' Mum shook her head. 'It was the best summer of my life.'

Anna and I were smiling. Talking about Cat like this would bring me closer to her memory, making contact easier. 'Keep going, Mum.'

'Then there was time I wanted to go to France. Catalina had been all over the world. She knowing what France look like. She take me there, in my head.' Mum pointed to her temple and sipped her tea.

'Wow,' I said. That was a skill I was still impressed with. Also one that, unfortunately, I never got to try with Cat.

'It was like I was there, Modesta. I could smell

the streets of Paris – not too lovely in some places, I telling you! I could feel the wind on my face. I hear peoples speaking in French. I could taste food and touching the water in the De La Concorde Fountain. All the time, I was lying on my beds.' Mum giggled.

'Cat took me in an aeroplane. A pretend one.' Anna nodded.

'Really?' I said.

'Yep. I was terrified to fly. I'd never done it and never wanted to,' Anna said. 'Anyway, I was wanted in Perth for a three-day professional development course, and I wasn't gonna drive across Australia, so Cat helped me with my fear. She had me on the sofa at home, and had conned me into trying it. So I did. It was so real.' Mum nodded in agreement as Anna spoke. 'I could hear the engine, and feel it tremble under me as we rolled along the runway. I could see the people around me strapped into their seats. She took me through the whole experience. When I woke up, I wasn't cured – but I knew what to expect. It hadn't been that bad. On the contrary, lift-off was quite exhilarating.'

I was in awe. 'She was amazing, wasn't she?'

'You remind me of her a lot, Mouse,' said Anna. 'I wouldn't be surprised if by the time you hit thirty, you'll know just as much as Cat did.'

I shook my head. 'I'll never be that powerful.' I had to wonder, were there things Cat could do that Mum and Anna never knew about? If she had been so similar to me, then wouldn't she have been exploring to see how far she could actually go? 'I've tried to push myself, but I don't get far, do I, Anna?'

She frowned at me.

'Sometime, things happen,' said Mum. 'And we become things we never think we can be.'

'Cheers to that,' said Anna. We clinked our teacups together. I felt warm and at peace, under the circumstances, and so it was the perfect time to take my bath and see if I could make contact with my aunty.

'So, before I do this, is everyone cool if I leave the bathroom door open?'

Mum and Anna nodded in unison. They didn't laugh at me. I loved them for that. The psycho witch-hag had me shaken. I'm sure her ugly face and feral, snake-tongue wouldn't leave my mind's eye for a long time. I could use the main bathroom, too. If there *was* a bath in my en-suite, I wouldn't have used it anyway. That door was shut tight for now.

It wasn't long before I was soaking in a mugwort, cinnamon, and star anise tub – with the bathroom door as open as it could get. When it came to Mum, Anna, and me, nudity had never been an issue.

I hopped into the tub, closed my eyes, and relaxed. I let the water take me in.

'Cat? What do I need to know?' I waited and breathed slowly and deeply. I took the air into my diaphragm as Anna had taught me, and each time I exhaled, I went deeper into a meditative state. Before long, I was gone.

My front steps groaned as I made my way over

to the Samson's old house. The Samson's had two younger children, and it had been refreshing to hear them playing outside all the time, climbing trees, riding skateboards, occasionally calling out to me to chat from the balcony. I knocked on the door and waited, half expecting Jessie Samson to poke her head through with a toothless grin and her effervescent giggle, carting her toy Totoro around everywhere she went.

There was nothing.

I couldn't quite recall what I was doing there. Maybe I had a babysitting job. I knocked again. Still nothing. I turned to leave, and the door creaked open. My breath caught in my throat. 'Hi,' I said.

A guy around my age stood there. His caramel eyes took me in. He leaned up against the door, chocolate locks pulled back into a ponytail, with a line of white hair, like Rouge from X-Men. He wore a Cradle of Filth T-shirt, revealing a naked nun hanging off his tall, lean body. He was the kind of guy I'd steer clear of in a dark alley.

'I'm Hamish.' It was a surfer's name, or a red-headed Scotsman's. Not this olive-skinned guy.

'I'm Mouse. I live next door.'

He shook my hand firmly, and grinned. 'Mouse?'

'It's short for Modesta.' I realised I was still holding onto him and tried to pull my hand away, but Hamish held on for a moment longer. Our skin was almost the same colour. 'Who are you?' I said, backing away. 'Where's Jessie Sampson?'

'Who are you?' He frowned. 'You knocked on my door.'

'No.' I shook my head. 'You're wrong.' We were standing in MY doorway. He'd knocked on MY door.

Hamish looked down, confused. 'Jessie Sampson is gone,' he said. 'How did I get here?' He looked scared.

Hamish's face morphed.

I was looking at Trent, now. I was sitting on my board in the water. We waited for the set to come in. I fell into the cool ocean with a splash and it soothed my burning skin. When I came back up, Trent was still sitting on his board, looking out over the flat water.

'I don't know why I'm here,' he said.

'What do you mean?' I asked. I surveyed the beach and it was all new to me. It wasn't Burleigh, or Miami. It wasn't Kirra Beach or any beach I knew.

'Are we lost?' I said.

Trent turned to me and his eyes were black pits. They were holes filled with darkness, and that darkness extended. A shadow the size of a fishing boat floated beneath me. The ocean turned grey and I could smell dead fish. There was blood on my tongue.

'They need you,' said Trent. 'Under the water.'

I screamed.

'Modesta!' Mum shouted. She and Anna leaned over me with horror-stricken faces. 'Wake up!'

It took a second for me to realise where I was. The water spilled over me as I pulled myself up. They grabbed my arms to help me out. Mum threw a towel around me.

'What happened? You were screaming,' Anna said.

'Damn. I feel asleep. It was just a nightmare. How long was I out?' I said.

'About five minutes. We'll let you get dressed.' Anna touched Mum on the arm.

'No, I'm okay,' I said. 'I've had worse nightmares than that before. Thanks, though.'

Anna rubbed my shoulder. 'All right. She's okay, Connie. Come on. We'll have another tea.'

When I got out of the bath, and dressed, I made my way out the front of the house. Sure enough, the Sampson's Jeep was still in their driveway. I'd have to keep an eye on Jessie.

I woke to the soft bells of my phone-alarm. I reached over and checked the time. 4:45AM. *Surf with Trent.* The day before came rushing back, and I wish I'd just woken up to realise it never happened.

But it had.

However, the worry was diminishing. I rolled over and pulled myself out of bed, careful not to wake Anna, who had taken the fold-out couch in the living room. I padded across the wooden floor toward the kitchen. I grabbed a banana, a bottle of water, and a beach towel and threw them into my bag. My journal sat in the bottom. I'd jotted down last night's tub nightmare, and hoped there would be nothing more to write about today.

I slowly opened the back door, and closed it as gently as I could. I made my way downstairs to our giant laundry area where I found my spare toothbrush, towel, and bikini, and got myself ready for a surf. My wetsuit was dry as a bone. Things didn't stay wet long in summer around here. You could dry your clothes on the line in half an hour. By 4:56AM I was on my Townie, bike helmet on, bag on back, and board under my arm, headed for the beach. It was hard to ride with a longboard at first, but I was a pro now. Well, for someone who was kind of uncoordinated. I could surf and I could dance, but that was as far as my physical capabilities went. Whenever there was a ball, it seemed repelled by me. I worried about it, since I was set to be a teacher. Trent joked that as long as I only taught up to grade two Phys. Ed., I'd be fine. I'd promptly punched him.

I smiled at the thought of Trent. It was a relief I would be able to tell him all about yesterday. He wouldn't even flinch. Well, he would, but he knew about my visions.

'Morning, sunshine.' I parked my bike near Trent. He sat on the grass, looking out at the water. The same spot he'd occupied every surf-meet for the past five years.

'Mornin',' he called back, as I put a chain on my bike tyre.

'Looks good,' I said as I surveyed the surf. Even if it was as flat as a pancake, we always went in for a swim, at least.

'Indeed it does.' He stood and gave me a hug. He held on tight, then pulled away to study me. 'What's up, chicken? You look like crap run over twice.'

'Thanks,' I said. 'I'm fine. A little tired, but I'll tell you about my awesome weekend so far when we're done.'

'That good, huh?'

I nodded. 'Worse.' We picked up our boards and made our way straight to the water. It was one of the things I loved about Trent: he got on with it.

I was glad we were going in from the shore instead of the rocks. I could leave my stuff on the sand in full view. Plus my hands were still a little sore. I had a few water-proof band-aides on them now. I felt another pang of guilt for lying to Trent. He'd know the truth soon enough.

There was no one out except a small group of people doing Tai Chi on the sand. I watched them for a moment. Things felt peaceful. I saw Trent paddle out, and in that moment, I felt as if everything was going to be okay. I was surrounded by people in my life who loved me. I smiled as he caught a few shoreys waiting for me to come out. I nodded and carried my longboard down to water's edge. The cool liquid splashed over my legs. When I was deep enough, I put my board down and went under to wet my hair.

The set was in and Trent was already attempting

the waves. He pulled himself up and immediately fell. I laughed.

I went under one more time.

As I came up and took a breath, I froze. My board was washed away by a wave, and the cord pulled tight at my leg.

The body of a young boy floated before me. His greying lips and blue skin suggested he'd been dead a while. He didn't sink to the bottom as a dead body with no air left in the lungs should. He just floated. The waves didn't move him either. I stared, and my heart seemed to freeze momentarily when I realised who he was.

Sonny.

He floated right before me now, and although I wanted to call for help, I knew he wasn't real. No one else could see the lifeless boy before me. I was the only *lucky* one.

I reached out to the little brother of my best friend, floating dead before me. His beautiful face was now blue and sagging, water-logged.

Then Sonny, the dead Sonny, took a gulp of air into his lungs and gasped for breath. I jumped and moved toward him. 'Sonny?' I whispered, careful not to let onlookers suspect I was completely nuts, talking to myself in the ocean. Not that I cared too much at this point. Sonny had his breath back but no colour returned to his lips. 'Sonny? What happened?'

He opened his mouth, but no words came – there was just a great black hole where his tongue should've been. I held the back of his neck as the set came in and started to throw us about. 'Sonny?'

He coughed and spluttered, and something came out of his mouth. I grabbed it. It was a silver pendant necklace, with a cross and circle at the top. I had seen it before somewhere.

The next wave hit us hard, and we both went under. My hands grasped for him, but I could no longer feel him in my grip.

I came up for air and Sonny was gone.

'Damn it!' I yelled. I grabbed my board and paddled back in.

'Mouse! What's wrong?' Trent followed me up the beach.

My arm was around my longboard, my other hand clasping so tightly to the pendant it almost drew blood. The pendant had *stayed*. The pendant hadn't disappeared in the visita, like it *should* have. I looked at my fist and was reminded of the small cuts on my hands that shouldn't have been there either. I couldn't cry, I couldn't speak. I just had to go. I had to be away from Trent before I turned around and told him what I just saw.

Please, no. Not Sonny. God damn it! I'd known him since the day he was born.

I'd been able to see the death of strangers and put a stop to it for so many years now, and I'd learned to live with it. Well, not just live with it, but to do something about it. Not just because there was an apparent punishment if I didn't, but because I couldn't live with myself otherwise. I'd been able to keep myself relatively detached. *This* wasn't a stranger, though. This was a friend. A small, innocent friend, who deserved nothing but ice cream and Superman figurines.

It made no sense. How could Sonny drown? He was a nipper. A talented swimmer and surfer.

'What happened, Mouse. Stop! For Chrissake!' Trent tried to grab me around the middle, but my board was in the way. I almost hit him with it.

'No!' I dropped everything and pushed him away. 'Leave me alone.'

He held my shoulders and I tried to pull away.

'I saw you,' he shouted. 'You had a vision, Mouse. It's all right. I'm here.' This time he won and pulled me in. He held me tightly.

Then the tears did come.

Mouse's Journal
My seventh visita - 25th June, 2013 at 2:35PM. English Class.

I froze over in English class, lucking out as it was during a movie. A little girl around four years old came to me battered and broken to the point of no return. She held shards of blue crockery. She wore a frilly dress, as if someone had made her into a living-doll, and she cried black tears. I reached out to soothe her, but then I was in her room, rather than block E at Miami High School, and she was showing me her fuzzy pink toys. Frilly Dress was so small, I wanted to pick her up and hold her. At first, her room smelled of candy and dirty washing.

The smoke alarms went off. I started as water poured from the ceiling, but I couldn't feel it. I couldn't feel in a visita. I could see, I could smell, and

I could hear, but not feel. I could smell something burning.

Frilly Dress pointed with her pudgy little arm, and made me look out the window. I saw her street address, VICTORIA STREET. How would I ever find that? I looked around for clues - tree types, building types, nothing looked familiar. I looked back at her and shook my head. She turned and reached under her tiny purple bed and pulled out her crayons and colouring book. She wrote on the page neater than I ever could - like she was a 70-year-old woman who had practised cursive her whole life. When I look back, I'm sure Frilly Dress wasn't the real messenger. I'm sure none of them were. How else could she have written like that? It read:

VICTORIA STREET, MELBOURNE.

I nodded.

I thought I'd need to eventually save this girl from a fire, considering the smell, yet she wasn't burned. They often came to me with markings of their death - and her markings were of beatings and scalds. Sure enough, it wasn't a fire. It was a thunderstorm, with water coming from the sprinkler system in the ceiling, and the thunder in the form of a size-eight woman. She thumped up the stairs. She stood in the doorway, screaming about burnt dinner, and how it was Frilly Dress's fault, somehow.

She walked right through me. She leaned over her little girl, and slapped her, leaving a red mark on those pink chubby cheeks and a tear-streaked face. The screaming started. I watched as the woman picked up a lamp; as it came crashing toward Frilly Dress. Blue shards. I snapped back to reality. I wasn't able to concentrate on the rest of that English lesson. I never did find out what happened to Elizabeth. I assume she married Darcy.

Trent and I made an anonymous phone call to DOCS after that. Frilly Dress's name was Samantha Cruise. She now lived at 44 Rock Street in Newcastle with a lovely foster carer named Doreen Straithfield, who'd adopted her along with another girl named Edie. She was nine.

CHAPTER 5

MY STOMACH ROILED. The people doing Tai Chi seemed to slow down. I was trying to hold it together as Trent and I sat on the grass. He had an arm around me. I was sure it was so I wouldn't run again. I played with the pendant.

'Was it as bad as Frilly Dress?' he said softly.

'Worse,' I finally said. 'It was worse than Frilly Dress. Worse than Green Pants. Worse than...'

He nodded. 'Look. Let's go and have a dirty-big bacon and egg hamburger from Sadies' and when you feel like talking, we'll talk. Whaddya say?'

I nodded. It was hard to see after so many tears, and Trent led me to the showers. We washed our boards, and feet, and put our longboards into Trent's van. *Abby's Mobile Soup Kitchen* was painted in cursive script along the side. We returned to get my Townie and put it inside the van, too.

Trent put an arm around me, and we made our way across the street. His warm body propped me up. He kissed the side of my head, brushing his nose in my wet hair as we walked.

The sound of the ocean and cawing gulls could still be heard at Sadie's. There were a few early-birds sitting in booths, and there were flags all around in ready for the Australia Day celebrations. Celebrating was the last thing I felt like doing.

Some customers looked as if they were just catching the bus in from a long hard night out at Surfer's Paradise, and others were standing by in their sporty shoes and outfits. Both groups would order a 'health' shot or smoothie – one to revitalise, and one to bring back the dead.

The smell of coffee and sound of sizzling bacon was familiar – like home. Huddled in my favourite booth, I felt a little safer than I had just moments ago. I no longer felt exposed, like a baby turtle on his way to the sea. I only hoped it wasn't a false sense of security.

Trent ordered our bacon and egg burgers and I watched him pay the young female clerk. She smiled at him with a sparkle in her eye. *Tough luck there, honey.*

The realisation of having to tell him the truth hit

me. How was I going to do this? I supposed the best way would be fast, like ripping off a band-aide. And the redeeming part of the story was Sonny could be saved. *Would* be saved. He wasn't dead yet. Someone up there, or something, wanted him alive. And I was damn-well going to do everything in my power to make sure that happened.

A tidal wave of feeling swept me under.

Heavy. Boggy. Crap. My head swirled. Maybe my body was reacting to stress.

I felt electricity in the air, static. I heard a sound like a thousand swarming bees. I looked down at my hands for some reason. Was this another vision? *Please, no.* I didn't sign up for this. In all honesty, I wouldn't have wished this 'gift' upon my worst enemy at the moment.

'Water, Hamish, darling. Quick sticks.' Her voice came from behind me. It sounded smooth to the ear, but when I heard it, it *felt* hard, rough, old. I didn't have to turn around to know it was *her*. I listened as someone got her a bottle of water from the fridge.

My fingers prickled, my heart thudded, my throat tightened, and I began to pant. I found it hard to swallow. If I looked up now, I'd see those eyes, and that auburn hair. *Come on, Mouse. Look at her. Calm yourself, harden up, and look at her!*

Perhaps that was Cat here now. I was too out of touch to tell. I glanced up.

I saw a taupe blouse and vanilla trousers over shapely legs. On the dark brown silky hair that fell to her waist was a floppy, navy blue sunhat. Hair no longer red, probably courtesy of L'Oreal.

There was a young man beside her. While she was facing the counter, he was leaning against it and facing *me*. His caramel eyes took me in. His arms were folded across an Escape the Fate T-shirt – the joker one, with the monkey on his shoulder. *Hamish.* The guy from my dream. The way he looked at me made my skin crawl – like he was wondering how to cook me and what I'd taste like.

'We've just arrived in town. I'm Aidah Armstrong, and this is my son, Hamish,' the woman said to the clerk.

'Hi,' the young girl said. She seemed uncomfortable. It was too much information. No one introduced themselves like that anymore.

Trent slid into the booth across from me. 'Mouse, you're so white you're green. Are you gonna puke?'

I finally swallowed and shook my head. 'No, I'm…' What was I? Okay? Definitely not that. My hands shook and Trent noticed. He lay his over mine to stop the tremble.

Trent respected my silence as I listened to Aidah chat to the creeped-out waitress about her son, and how they'd just driven in from Sydney. Trent pushed a banana smoothie toward me.

Aidah and Hamish paid for their water, a pack of gum, and some Curly Wurlys. When they turned to walk out, Aidah pulled down her shades. I couldn't see her eyes, but I knew that face anywhere. It was the face from my mirror.

My heart seemed to stop like a light shutting off. On its retuning beat, which seemed as if it would never come, Hamish stared at me again. This time he frowned. I looked away. What did he see? Did he know who I was, what I saw? The last thing I wanted was to be on the radar of those two.

'Trent. This is going to seem crazy,' I whispered as they strolled out the door of Sadie's, 'but you've known me for a long time and you know I'm not insane. Hopefully.' *Trent, I'm pretty sure this lady is a witch who wants to kidnap children, and one of them could be your little bro, but just chill, 'cause we got this.*

'What did you see, Mouse.' He put a hand over mine.

'Sonny,' I said. It was all I could manage.

There was a long pause. 'You saw Sonny.' His voice wavered. 'Where? How?'

'He was in the water in front of me. He was…' I had to come right out and say it or I never would, 'drowned.'

Trent's face twisted up. 'No.' He stared at me. 'No.'

'It hasn't happened yet. All right? It doesn't have to happen.'

Trent nodded. 'You're right. That's what you do, you stop this. That's why you were shown it, so you can stop it.' He was talking fast, and becoming hysterical. 'You have to stop this, Mouse. We can't let this happen!'

'Calm down,' I said. 'We can fix this, but I need

you to breathe.' We were now shaking like leaves at the top of an exposed branch in a wind-storm.

Trent complied. After a few breaths, he was coming to his senses. 'Okay, so he never goes in the ocean without us. I don't understand how this could even happen. Was there a rip?' I shook my head, thinking of the best way to tell him what was on my mind. 'What was he wearing?'

'What?'

'In the vision, what did he have on?'

'Um. Some kind of red swimmers,' I said. They had definitely been red. I saw them, bright on his pasty flesh. That vision of Sonny Albright would never leave me.

Bright red. Lime green. Frilly dress. Snaky-tongues. Har de har.

Trent seemed to be thinking. 'He doesn't have red swimmers. Are you sure it was him? He's a champion junior nipper. I mean, you know. You've been under a lot of stress lately. Are you worried about these uni assignments?'

'I...'

'The only time he swims at Burleigh Beach is with all of us there, Mouse. He's not allowed near the water otherwise. I just don't see it happening. It *had* to be someone else.' Trent was in denial – understandably.

'I think someone is going to...' I couldn't go on.

Trent's face changed from fear to anger. 'What? Someone's going to what?'

'To hurt him.' This was going from bad to worse.

'Who? Who's going to hurt him?' His face was red. I saw the whites of his knuckles as he clenched his other fist.

'If you take me home, I'll tell you everything,' I said.

'Does it have something to do with these people you were just eye-balling? You looked terrified at the sight of them,' he said.

I looked him in the eye, and for the second time in our twelve-year friendship, I lied again. 'No, Trent. It has nothing to do with those people. I thought they were someone else.' Trent put his burger down, and came over to my side of the booth to embrace me. This time *he* let out a sob or two. My bestie was tough, but he could cry like the rest of us. After all, he knew my visions were real, and he had family at stake.

'I'll take care of my little brother. Thank you.' He kissed my cheek. 'This won't be another Hank.' If there was one positive thing about having Trent as a bestie, it was that he went through his emotions quickly, came to his senses in moments, and acted with logic immediately.

'No more Hanks,' I said. Hank hadn't been as lucky as my others.

I couldn't tell Trent about Aidah, or Sacmis, or whatever the hell-spawned thing from my visita had called itself, because he'd take his eyes off Sonny, and that couldn't happen. Not only that, he'd probably play hero, and go and get himself killed instead. 'You need to take care of your family,' I said. I couldn't bear to think about losing a single Albright, let alone two.

I had to find out where this Aidah and Hamish were living. I HAD to talk to Cat.

CHAPTER
6

I WAS LYING STILL on my bed. I needed a hot shower.
I needed a brain wipe. I needed to take all the horrible
sights I have seen in my life so far and throw them off
some cliff somewhere far away. I'd rather be normal.
Read a book and sip some tea, normal. Meet a boy
and catch a movie, normal.

This whole seeing dead people before they were
dead, changing the future, and saving lives – this
whole superhero thing I had going on – I wanted to
be done. I wanted to hang up my cape. No, I wanted
to set the bloody thing on fire, and throw the ashes
into Heard Volcano, while singing 'free at last.' I rolled
over and covered my head with my pillow, blocking
out the sound and light.

Trent had gone home to be with Sonny. 'He'll be fine now that we know, Trent,' I had convinced him. 'Almost every vision I've ever had allowed me to change the future.' We had sat in his van out the front of my house for a while before he left. He hadn't let me ride my bike home after how shaken up I was.

'Someone up there is looking out for us,' he had whispered as he kissed my cheek.

'Right, and you need to give me some space so I can work my magic, all right? I promise to call you later.' He had been satisfied with that and let me go. I'd been lying on my bed all morning, trying to figure out what to do. I uncovered my face before I smothered myself, and I sat up.

Then another face appeared in my mind's eye. Not Aidah's. Her son's. What was his name? Hamos? Hamish. That was it.

The way he'd looked at me like I was a hot dog…

I took out my journal. I reread the dream I had with Hamish coming to the door at the Sampson house. He had been kind in the dream. In real life, not so much.

I pulled the pendant out of my pocket. *Sonny's little gift.* I ran my finger over the arc. A little shock bolted through me, like I'd touched a live wire. *Zap.* I dropped the pendant on the bed. Conscious of the shock, I tapped the pendant and drew my hand away fast in case it got me again. I did it two more times before realising it wasn't going to sting a second time. Probably just static electricity.

I put the pendant onto a chain, and then around my neck. It seemed like the natural thing to do. A cross with a circle. My wiccan spells and symbols book told me it was an 'ankh.' It had been right on the tip of my tongue. Cat would've booted me in the butt if she'd known I'd forgotten it.

Life.

Why had a dead Sonny come to me with the symbol for life?

I pulled out the set of tarot cards Anna had given me for my fifteenth birthday. *Come on. Give me something.* A photo of Cat sat beside me. A white candle still burned on my bedside table and the woodsy aroma of sandalwood incense filled the room. I placed a catlinite stone in the centre. 'Cat? I don't know if these cards will help, but I know you can hear me. I don't know what I'm supposed to do. All I have is this ankh. Please help.' I exhaled.

I put my hand in a bowl of water on my bedside table, of which had produced no results earlier, and kept it there as I swirled my tarot cards around on my bed with my free hand. I closed my eyes and let them be drawn to the cards. A tingle drew me to a card, and I turned it over. 'Okay, The Moon. Nothing is as it seems. Got it.' I jumped as the card flapped around the room like an unseen force had picked it up and was dancing with it. 'Cat, why can't you just talk to me like you usually do?'

Another card flew up and hit me on the nose. 'The Hermit. Hmmm. Loneliness, withdrawing, silence.' I thought for a moment. 'You can't. You can't tell me because you're bound? No, that's not it.'

All the cards separated from two in the centre, which turned over. The first was Death. The second was Judgment. Anubis stood on the Death card holding a golden vase. The scales stood behind him at the 'weighing of the souls.' Anubis then ushered souls to the afterlife.

'Afterlife. Life. Death. You and Anna always taught me Death was a good card, a card of change and growth. And Judgement?' I got up to write the two cards down. 'This might take me some time.' I looked up at the roof as if she'd be there, 'I don't have time, Cat. You've gotta help me sooner.' Frustrated I kneeled on the bed and gathered the cards up. 'Maybe you can't talk to me because you're afraid the wrong person will hear.'

My legs wobbled. My vision blurred. I fell backward onto the floor.

The waves crashed, and the sun beat down like seven hells. The furnace heat and the cawing gulls urged me to wake, but I couldn't sit up yet. I was too heavy and groggy. Had I fallen asleep sunbathing again? Damn! I'd be fried like an egg. I rubbed my arms. They were burnt, but fortunately, I wasn't too crispy. My first day of prac was coming up, and I didn't want to go in looking like a giant

lobster squeezed into its Sunday Best – a burnt teacher giving sun-safety talks wasn't a good look.

My mind filled with a hissing sound, like a pressure cooker on high, and I grabbed at my temples. I sat up.

What was that?

I looked down to see my black pants, Converse shoes, and a red top. The kind of thing I wore all the time, but never to the beach. I couldn't think straight. Come on, Mouse, think. What's going on? Hadn't I just been in my bedroom?

My bottom felt like it was in cement, rather than sitting in the sand, and my muscles ached as I pulled myself up. Walking felt like I was in one of those dreams where you were about to be chased by something terrifying, and then BAM! Low and behold, you couldn't run anywhere, because for some unknown reason, you forgot how to use your legs. Awesome.

The surf was empty, and that's when I realised, I was in a visita again. Okay, I could handle this. Right? I prayed to God, some God, somewhere, that Sonny Albright wouldn't show up again with his bloated tummy and blue lips, spitting out objects at me to wear as jewellery. I looked around for him all the same. There was nothing happening. Even the gulls I'd heard when I woke up were gone.

The blast-furnace breeze slapped my face, and the sand pelted my raw arms like buckshot.

It hurt.

If this was the shape of things to come for me, where my visions could get dangerous, I really didn't want them anymore.

I checked my pocket for my phone. It was nine AM. There should be plenty of people around by now. Exercise freaks should be tearing along the sand in Lorna Jane shorts and bikini tops, sizing up the other exercise freaks. Then there should've been sunbathers, and people swimming. The red and yellow lifeguard flags should have already been set up, too.

But the place was deserted.

Usually, I'd see everything in future 'real time.'

I checked my phone again, and six missed calls and a message from Trent popped up:

Mouse, where are you? Are you okay?

Two excellent questions. *I trotted up the beach, and I looked around for someone, anyone, with no luck.*

I got to the highway – no cars, either.

Was this the end of the world I was seeing? Some re-enactment of The Stand? *Had the air been polluted with a toxin that had taken out the Gold Coast population? Surely I'd see bodies, and even a gist of what went on, so I could stop it.*

The hissing returned, this time stronger. A kettle boiled in my head.

'What is this!?'

The hissing stopped and was replaced with whispers.

Ven a mí, Ven a mí.

It was my own voice in Spanish. Come to me, *it said.*

'Cat? Where?' This didn't feel good. Cat always did. Her messages came with a sense of lightness and wellbeing.

A little girl moved out from behind a tree. Her skin was pale and bloated like Sonny's was when I found him in the water. Her eyes were swollen and sad. Long wet hair clung to her cheeks and the closer I got, the more she looked like me.

Me as a child.

Me as a drowned child. She opened her mouth and her two front teeth were missing. She pointed down the street. I tried to talk to her but my mouth wouldn't open. She shook her head sadly and continued to point until I moved past.

The windows of the empty houses grew, the nothingness inside made plain. I was on Christine Avenue standing before a house. The house with the cream walls and an electric gate. I couldn't recall how it was significant to me. When I tried to reach for a memory, there was nothing there. I was looking for a light-switch that somebody had moved in the dark.

A deep loneliness crept over me. A sorrow. Someone else's sorrow. I walked and I cried. Melancholy swallowed me up to the point where it was hard to see. My body wailed with sadness, weights of death and loss heavy on my chest, sweaty, strong hands around my throat. I couldn't breathe!

'¡Deteneos! *Stop! Do not kill her.*' It wasn't my voice. 'An eye for an eye.'

I was choking now. My throat was on fire from the pain. I fell to my knees, and they hit the cement path so hard, my kneecaps tore from my legs. The blood! The agony. My trembling body was lifted into the air. My hands tore at the unseen hands at my throat. If I didn't get air soon, I'd be dead. Dead as Aunt Catalina. Dead as Sonny Albright. Dead as – the fire started, pocking my tortured skin with deep, ghastly burns. Death, a former enemy, would now be the friend to release me from this impossible suffering.

I was almost gone. At least I'd get to see Cat again. We could look after Mum and Anna from a distance. We could make sure Sonny never went near the water again.

I was falling, and finally, the pain subsided. Let go.

MODESTA !

The ankh around my neck felt cold.

'En la oscuridad, donde reside el mal, invoco la luz en mi corazón.'

She chanted...or someone did.

I didn't know what it meant, but I memorised the words. They resonated over and over, and I chanted, too. The ankh burst open. Water poured over my burning body. The relief was instant.

I fell to the hard ground.

I woke on the floor. When I sat up my head pounded. More pain. My visions were making no sense and they were coming at me faster than ever. I checked my knees. They were fine. I pulled myself up onto my bed and opened my top bedside drawer. I filled a small crystal sack. 'Agate, protection, celestite, guidance. Elestial to uncover secrets, calcite to reduce fear and make me invisible,' I whispered as I put the sack into my pocket. 'By the light of day, I'm dark as night. Keep me safe and out of sight.' I sent a prayer up to my deity, Criede, and hoped she was listening.

Someone on Christine Avenue was about to get a visit.

CHAPTER 7

THE BIRDS' INCESSANT SQUAWKS were rivalled only by the pervasive auto exhaust as I made my way to Christine Avenue by foot. Since I'd made my decision to spy on our psycho-neighbour and her son, I'd been in such a rush to get dressed I'd only just noticed what I had on.

Cons, black pants, red top.

I shrugged. Changing your clothes wouldn't stop the future from happening but the thought of the pain in my last visita still caused a knot in my throat and butterflies in my belly.

I clung to the crystal sack in my pocket, thinking about the little girl with the missing teeth in my vision, the one who looked like me. Holding my breath as I walked past the tree she'd appeared behind, I watched the spot. She never came.

P-plater cars hooned past with people yahooing. A guy with the Australian flag painted down his face stuck his head out of the passenger side window and called, 'Hey, baby!'

I shook my head, 'no.' He stuck his middle finger up at me. *Very Aussie. And up yours too, mate.*

The house was ahead. I couldn't be sure if it belonged to Aidah and Hamish. All signs pointed that way. Mum's words 'look for the signs' echoed in my head and I was able to convince myself I wasn't that crazy.

I'd never get over that electric gate without being noticed, so I ducked around the side of the house next door, hoping my prayer and crystals would keep me invisible. I had to believe strongly in my craft today – one must believe it strongly every day – but I sometimes fell short, just a little. There were times I just sucked it up and did what had to be done.

I wished Trent was with me. Not only would he make me feel a whole lot safer, he could boost me over the fence I was trying to climb. I finally pulled myself up onto the fence and checked for fierce, undead, demon guard dogs, before throwing my leg over. *No dogs, check.* I landed, rather ungracefully, on the other side. I stood too quickly and my ankle gave way and twisted.

I fell.

Too bad if Aidah decided to chase me now. I'd be dead three times over.

This seemed like a really bad idea now that I was

here. Courage went on a break for a second. I closed my eyes and took a deep breath. Sonny's dead face appeared behind my closed eyes, and I'd be damned if I was going to let some witch-hag from out of town take my bestie's little brother without a fight – one of us was going down – and it was all right if it was me. Aidah would still have Anna, Mum, Trent, and Rick and Carey Albright to get through. And Nanna Albright, too.

I edged along the side of the house and peered into a window. Luckily it was only one level, or then I'd *really* be in trouble. Tree-climbing was not my thing. I'd never make a great stalker. It was easy to see into their living room. Boxes lined the walls. They had old, mismatched sofas and tatty artwork. It looked like Aidah and Hamish were collectors. What they'd unpacked looked antique, including the ornate, framed pieces of jewellery they had already put up on the walls. *Jewellery.* I grabbed the ankh on my neck, half expecting it to have disappeared. It was still there.

I caught a glimpse of Hamish. *There. It is your place.* He came into the living room, and I side-stepped out of view. I waited a moment then ventured another look. He started to unpack some boxes. *Nothing unusual here.* I crept along the side of the house. Maybe I'd see Aidah. *Oh, hey, I'm your new neighbour. Don't mind me. It's protocol to peep through each others' windows at random intervals.*

Most of the curtains were closed along the side of

the house. I went to make my way around the back. There she was.

My breath caught in my throat. She was sunbathing in a lie low by a pool, reading something. Her body was perfectly sculpted and tanned – not really the hag from my vision, but she had started out beautiful hadn't she – before her disgusting tongue invaded my ear?

Aidah still wore her gigantic sunnies and floppy hat. I had no funny vibes. Either the celestite and elestial weren't working, or this was all something I had built up in my head, given energy to, and turned into a thing that wasn't an actual threat. Maybe Anna's reading the other day was picking up some old vibes that were benign. I clutched my crystals and focussed.

Still nothing.

This wasn't helpful at all. In fact, now that I was completely second-guessing myself, it was time to go home and re-group.

I turned and bounced right off of Hamish's chest!

He grabbed my wrists and demanded, 'What are *you* doing?' He dragged me back around the side of the house as I struggled to break free. 'You shouldn't have come here,' he growled, glaring. 'Are you insane?' He dropped my wrists as if they were coated in sewage.

'Uh … no.' I managed to say, rubbing the sore and bruised areas. 'And don't you ever touch me again, you psycho.'

'*Me*, the psycho? You're the…' He bit his lip. 'Never mind. Just leave.' He pushed a hidden button inside his pocket, and the gate opened. Hamish pointed to the exit.

'I'm already gone.' I stormed out, adrenaline pumping from both the fear of being caught and the relief from not being eaten by bruja and son. I heard the electric gate close after me as I power walked as fast as I could.

'Wait.' Hamish was suddenly behind me. I quickened my pace. 'Wait!' he said again as he ran up beside me. 'I can't *believe* I'm doing this.'

I stormed on. 'Go away,' I said. He grabbed me by the shoulder. 'I said, *don't touch me!*'

Then, I turned and punched him square in the forehead.

'Ouch!' we cried in unison. My ring left a bloody spot by his eyebrow and the whole top of his t-zone went bright red. He reeled forward and put a hand over his brow. My hand throbbed. I tried to stop him from falling forward, but to no avail. He fell to his knees on the grass by the footpath.

'Jesus Christ! Was that really necessary?' He gathered himself and got back up. He frowned at me, shook his head, and turned back towards his house.

'Hamish!' I called.

He turned, gave me that horrendous glare, and stormed back over. 'How do you know my name?'

'I … your mum, Aidah, said in the shop. To the girl at the counter.' I said. *Great, Mouse. Why don't you tell him everything you know?*

'Listen, I don't know who you are, or what your

deal is,' he said. 'But stay the hell away from me and my mother, you hear me?'

My throat tightened. I nodded. This seemed to be just some normal guy. His mother seemed normal, too. I was deflated like a limp balloon. I turned and made my way home.

'Anna?' I sat on my bed and played with the ankh around my neck.

'Hi, kiddo. Sorry I missed your call, I had my phone on silent. I don't know why it keeps doing that.' There was a long pause. 'How you doin'?'

'Not so great,' I said.

'Do you need me to come back over?' said Anna.

'No, it's not that, it's just … well.'

'Spit it out, Mouse. It's me here,' she said.

'I'm worried everything that's going on isn't quite right. I mean already it's *not right*, but all my visitas prior to today have been pretty clear, pretty straight-forward. I see something, I stop it from happening. The vision gives me the detail, like where and when, right?'

'Right,' she said. 'Slow down. Take your time so I can understand you.'

'Okay, sorry. So, I usually have a vision like once or twice a year. Now I'm having visions all over the place. There's no time indications, I just, I'm not used to having so little control.'

'What do you mean visions all over the place? There was the one with the woman in the mirror. That's all that's happened so far, Mouse, isn't it?'

I didn't answer.

'Mouse!'

'I feel like I'm going crazy,' I whispered.

'Modesta, I'm coming over.'

'No, that's just it. I'm all right. I feel like everything is just fine.'

Anna coughed. 'Really? Everything is just fine, but you're going insane.'

'Yeah, I think maybe I'm under a lot of stress from uni and I just need to relax a bit.' Anna didn't speak. She just breathed calmly on the other end. I was annoyed. 'Anna, say something.'

'Something.'

I laughed. 'Do you think everything is okay?' I said.

'I don't know, kiddo. I don't like what happened the other day Not one bit. That take-over and that reading I did. I'm going to school tomorrow to do some protection work. I still feel like something's off. You're off too. Maybe take it real easy, all right?'

'Yeah.' I thought of Sonny. It was his school, too. 'We can't be too careful. Whether it's all in my head or not, it's worth doing the protection spells. I'll help you.'

'Good girl.' Anna said. 'It's good practise, regardless. And a rite is more powerful with a coven. Connie can come, too.'

A sadness came. A rock-like feeling sat in the pit of my stomach. We were *supposed* to be a coven. Anna, Cat, Mum, and I, but it never came about.

'Mum isn't magic but,' I'd said to Cat when I was small.

'You don't say but at the end of a sentence, Mouse. No, Connie isn't magic in the way you are, or in the way Anna is,' she had said, as she was cooking me some rice. '*But,* everyone is magic, Modesta Castro, and don't you forget it. Now pass me the salt.' I smiled at the thought of Aunt Catalina making me her horrid, half-cooked rice. I'd eat it a thousand times over if I had the chance now.

'So,' I said to Anna. 'How much salt are you going to need to do an entire school?'

She chuckled. 'We don't need salt but we need a lot of chalk. I'm pretty sure we've got that covered.'

I rested like Anna told me to. That night I didn't dream.

Mouse's Journal
My fifth visita - 14th November, 2010.
Kitchen. Elder Entrance.

My class was practising 'Double Double Toil and Trouble,' upon request from our choir teacher, and I sang for Mum in the kitchen. I stopped as a man came to me. 'I'm here to cut the trees down out front,' he said. Blood clotted at his temple like he'd been dead a little while. He wore a bright green shirt, and still held part of his harness in his hands.

'Where are you?' I asked the usual question. He looked around, confused. 'Are you in Queensland?' I knew I had little time before he disappeared. Mum stayed silent, staring at me.

'We're a Melbourne-based business,' he said.

'How wonderful. What's the name of your business?'

Mum smiled at me and nodded

in encouragement. She knew I was having a vision. She had been through it with Cat.

'Jim's Services. You can call me Hank, though. I'm the son.'

'You're all right, Hank,' I said, before he disappeared.

Mum waited and when I gave the nod, she threw her arms around me. 'You did so good!' she said.

I repeated everything Hank had said and Mum went about calling up to find out about Jim's tree-lopping services in Melbourne. Hank and his family didn't listen to Mum's warning. His death was in the news the following day.

CHAPTER 8

'**THE STONES HAVE BEEN CHARGED** and will be placed at each corner of the school,' Anna said as she opened the boot of her car. Mum and I took a stone; it was more like a bolder. 'Chanting was used to charge them, Mouse. What kind do you think?' Anna was always teaching.

'White light protection?' I said. That's all it ever was lately.

'Good.' She nodded as she grabbed one of the stones and heaved it out. 'Inside these rocks are gemstones. Black onyx. It's not only a powerful protector, but the absence of light creates invisibility.'

THAT was the one I should've taken yesterday. Maybe then I wouldn't have had a literal run-in with

Hamish. The guilt crept over me for punching the poor guy in the face. I wondered how his forehead was today – whether I'd left a mark. My cuts had healed well and stung less but now my right hand ached as I carried the heavy stones. It *had* collided with a bone. He and Aidah could sue me for both trespassing, and physical abuse.

I tried to recall the bruja in the mirror from Saturday, and I tried to reimagine the feeling I got when I first saw Hamish and Aidah in Sadie's. The memory fluttered away like a butterfly over a fence. I knew it was there, but it was no longer in sight – no longer reachable. Memory could be fickle as the wind, especially when you needed it most.

'It should keep us under the radar,' Anna continued.

Mum huffed as we placed our stone down in the first spot by the garden – the east side. 'We protect this place,' she said between breaths, 'but this evil goes to another school. This evil goes to other children.'

'We can't protect everyone, Mum,' I said.

'I worry about that, too,' said Anna. 'Connie, the vision was for Mouse. This is where she'll be spending most of her time come tomorrow. And I just know if she needs to protect a child, she'll be shown more. It's the way of it.'

I bit my lip. I wanted to tell them about Sonny. Anna looked at me and for a moment I was worried she already knew. After yesterday, I felt like I was losing my touch – like I was making up stories in my head about some poor woman and her son who were new in town.

Cat, where are you? I shrieked in my mind to a ghost who'd stopped returning my calls. *I don't know what's real anymore.*

'Watchers of the east, keep us safe.' Anna used chalk to draw a half triangle, with a circle inside on the cement. Mum and I repeated her words. Anna pushed the stone over the glyph and we moved on. We placed our stones at the four corners of the school, and after Anna had finished her last chant, we made our way back to her car.

'Do you think this enough?' said Mum.

'For now,' said Anna. 'Mouse and I will do the house then she can get on with her schoolwork.' Anna studied me. 'We can go on as normal tomorrow, Modesta. Unfortunately being a witch while trying to lead a normal life means nothing stops in a crisis.'

'The show must go on,' I said.

When we got home Anna sent me around the house to do some smudging. I trailed bergamot around my room. I stepped into the en-suite for the first time since Saturday morning. 'Protect us with all your might, oh Goddess gracious day and night.' I stood before the mirror and waited. 'Nothing. She's nothing. It's nothing.' I smiled at my reflection. 'You got this, *Sirenita*.'

I continued my chant all the way around the house as Anna poured sea salt by the windows. I put my bergamot down, and Anna came over to me.

'Ankh. That's clever, Mouse,' she said as she studied my pendant. 'In some cases it's used for protection, even love. But why this particular one?' I shrugged. 'This is a different kind of ankh,' Anna said. 'It's used in ceremonies to resurrect the dead.' I tried to hide my shock. 'Where did you get it?' Anna seemed to look right through me.

'Sonny Albright gave it to me.' It wasn't a lie. Not technically. How could I be questioning everything when I still had this bloody thing around my neck?

'Just be careful what you do with it.' Anna passed me and went to join Mum in the living room.

After rummaging through the kitchen for a while and snacking on a bit of everything in the fridge, I found myself hungry still. When my heart was empty, I could never quite fill my stomach. I made my way to my bedroom.

Tomorrow I'd meet Ms Lawson again and start my internship. Thank goodness for the public holiday. While families spent their long-weekend relaxing at the beach, I got to work. It took most of the day, but I finished off my lesson plans, and then spent the next hour ironing clothes for the week. Anna had gone home for the night.

Mum was watching the news. I decided to pack my school lunch before making dinner. That's when Mum screamed. My apple fell to the kitchen floor. I ran to the lounge room.

'What! What is it?' I said. She pointed at the television.

'Megan Small went missing from her Gold Coast home sometime last night,' Bruce Paige from Channel Nine said.

The television cut to a distressed woman. The text beneath her read: Racheal Small, Megan's step mother.

'I don't know what time it happened. There was no forced entry,' she said. 'We heard nothing. We just want our little girl back.' Video footage of Megan came up on the screen. There were some clear shots of her face, her brown pigtails, and her missing teeth. She was receiving presents at her birthday party. As she tore open a present she whistled, and my skin crawled. It was to the tune of "Twinkle Twinkle Little Star."

It ended with a school photo of her. The uniform was too familiar. My stomach flipped. Everything I picked at in the kitchen threatened to revisit me. All went quiet. My legs gave out from under me and I fell to the floor.

'Modesta!' Mum called to me. She was by my side and helped me into a sitting position. My phone rang in my pocket. It was Anna.

'Anna?'

'Modesta. Did you see it?' she said. 'We're too late,' she said. 'Megan Small. She's gone missing.'

'She's one of your students,' I said.

'Yes. And she's one of yours, Mouse. She's supposed to be in your class tomorrow. She's a friend of Sonny's.'

Now my stomach really flipped. 'My class,' was all I managed to say.

'She's been gone all night. You didn't see anything, no visitas?' Anna said.

I could hardly hear her anymore. All I could hear was the whistling, *Twinkle Twinkle.* 'She puts her tongue in your ear,' I found myself saying. Then I passed out.

I heard Anna's voice. 'I compel you to tell me the truth.' I was in my bed. Wax burned my arm.

'Ouch!'

'Anna, do not hurt her. She been through enough!' Mum slapped Anna on the arm.

'I'll do more than that,' said Anna. I smelled thyme.

'What else have you seen, Modesta?' My tongue tingled, then it burned as if I had just chewed a Habanero pepper! 'Speak and the pain will subside,' Anna said calmly, as she and Mum sat on my bed.

'Tell her, young lady.' Mum pointed a finger at me. I needed the pain to stop.

Once the words started, they poured out like water. 'Sonny died in the ocean.' It started there, and ended with me talking to Hamish yesterday. When I stopped speaking, the burning was completely gone.

'Do you understand what this secret has done?' Anna asked.

I nodded. Tears came.

She stood and paced the room. When she saw how upset I was, she stopped. She sat back on my bed. 'I know, I know.' She hugged me. 'It's all right.'

Mum put her arm around me from the other side. 'It must be hard for you. You see little Sonny hurt,' Mum said.

'We've put our protection around the school. Once the students arrive tomorrow I'll do some more work. For now, we have to go and get Megan back,' said Anna.

'What?' Mum cried out. 'No, no, no. Neither of you go anywhere!' She stood.

'We have to,' I said. 'We have no choice.'

Anna nodded. 'Agreed.'

I thought about Aidah and Hamish. 'What if Aidah isn't responsible?'

Anna stared at me. She seemed to come to some realisation and a smile danced on her lips. She shook her head. 'I can't believe I didn't even think of it.'

'What?' I asked.

'She's done this. It's *her* fault,' Anna said. 'It's not your fault for keeping secrets, Mouse. Aidah makes you see her as she wants you to see her. Even *you*. She fooled even you! She dulled your senses.'

'Magic,' I breathed.

'Let me check. I'll get the knife.' Anna stood.

'What?' Mum jumped off the bed. 'No knives!'

'I've seen this before, Connie,' Anna huffed. 'The same glazed over look in the eyes, the off behaviour.' Anna pointed at me. 'When I was small, a horrid little slag called Brigid came to my school. She had everyone fooled into thinking she was an angel. Underneath? She was like Damien from *The Omen*, or Henry from *The Good Son.'* Anna started pacing again. 'Accidents started happening, parents went missing. One of the older kids Brigid didn't like walked off the edge of the Southport Peer and drowned! No one pointed a finger at her. Somehow, *I* was immune. I saw through, and I see through now! Around the time Brigid showed up, everyone got this dreamy look, like Modesta did when she mentioned Aidah. It's old magic.'

'If this is true,' said Mum, 'What must we do with the knife?'

Anna placed her hands on her hips. 'It's not for Mouse. It's for me.'

Mum threw her hands up. 'Well, why no say this?'

'I studied Brigid for days trying to figure out how she did it – made everyone stupid – I mean. No offence, Mouse. Until I realised all they need to do is breath the same air, and it can get into your lungs. Into the blood. Into the brain. Aidah will have everyone wrapped around her little finger without even trying. But not us. Like I said, I'll get the knife.'

Anna did the ceremony in the next room. She wanted to be alone for it, and I could learn another time, when the stakes weren't so high. I was cool with that. I may have seen plenty of blood in my lifetime, and Mum may work in a hospital, but when we had the choice, we'd prefer to be ignorant, thank you very much.

It was called a spell binding. It was an anti-spell, or shield, stopping Aidah from getting into our systems – *and* getting her out of mine at the same time. Anna had to cut her arm, and draw the blood down the blade. It was as effective as it was disgusting, in my opinion, and I'd have to learn how to do it sooner rather than later. She said my name and I heard it like she was next to me. My body tingled, sweat poured out even though I was stationary, and the room smelt of petrol. There was a fizzing sound in my ears, then a pop. 'I think it's working,' I said to Mum as she held my hand.

An azure blue mist cloaked us. Mum shivered. It felt like ice ran through my veins. Mum wrapped her arms around me as we breathed frost, and looked at each other with wide eyes. A little warning from Anna would've been nice, though she'd been so hyper, pacing all over the place like a monkey in a cage, it'd surely slipped her mind.

When Anna returned to my bedroom, Mum and I were warming back up. I'd gone from sweating, to freezing, and back to Gold Coast, summertime sticky, in the space of four minutes.

Anna had dried blood on her arm still. She hardly saw us, as she went on with her rant as if she'd never left the room. 'She's got people fooled into thinking she's some normal woman. I bet she's even the kind who attends meetings and organises charity events.'

'Anna!' I stood up, walked over to her, and squeezed

her shoulders. 'Calm down. You're not focussed. You could have told Mum and I we'd almost freeze to death with your spell. You're not even looking at me!' I shook her now.

She stared at me with empty eyes for a few seconds. '*Mitote*,' I said.

Anna took a deep breath. There was a re-entry of the self, back down to the earth-plane, and now she was *seeing* me. She nodded. '*Maya.*' We smiled at each other. Both words meant a fog of perception, a non-presence. Both were a reminder that we must awaken from our dreams, and return to the now. If you let them drive all the time, emotions were a powerful vehicle on the road to destruction.

'Back to Aidah,' I said as I returned to sit on my bed. 'I felt her at first. In Sadie's. I felt what was really under there. It was … nasty. There was a kind of heavy static in the air when she came in the room.'

Anna nodded. 'And this Hamish?'

I shrugged. 'I don't know. He seems like a normal kid. But Aidah started to look like a normal woman to me, too. My judgment is moot, I suppose.'

'It won't be now,' said Anna. She took the chair in my corner, covered in clothes. Mum sat quietly listening.

'I've found out as much as I could about this Sacmis who came to visit us the other day,' said Anna. 'These women are definitely connected. I'm thinking they're related. This confirms my thoughts. If this Aidah woman makes people think a certain way around her, it's similar to the story. Sacmis was able to make the villagers think things. As we've learned from little Brigid, it's dangerous. Really dangerous.'

I gasped and put a hand to my mouth. 'That's how she lures the children.'

'Probably.'

'How she lured Megan.' I was feeling sick again. 'I have to call Trent about Sonny.'

'You do,' said Anna. 'Trent can't let him out of sight. Tomorrow at school, we'll do a protection spell. We can do it without his noticing. Connie, I need you and Modesta to stay here, do you both understand?' said Anna.

'Oh hell no!' I stood. 'I'm coming, too. Besides, I'm the one who knows where Aidah lives.'

'Well, we go nowhere without a plan,' said Mum. She stood and put her hands on her hips. 'You all listening to me. I have the plan. I know exactly what your Aunty Catalina would do. Okay?'

Anna smiled and nodded. 'Okay, Connie. Who are we to argue with that? Mouse, welcome to the magic of Connie Castro. Watch and learn.'

CHAPTER 9

MUM STOOD OVER A BOX that sat on her bed. 'Is in here.' She pointed at it.

I swallowed. 'Okay. Who's doing the honours?'

Anna stared at the box. 'You should do it, Connie.'

Mum nodded and opened the box. I stared. 'It's hideous.'

'It's beautiful,' Anna said as she studied the crude, carved giraffe. 'It's obviously African.'

'*Sí*,' said Mum. 'It was given to Catalina from Mali. Witch doctors. He say it help her see far.'

'The Mali worship *Ama*.' Anna was getting excited, which meant she had facts to share. 'Divination and healing. There's no dark magic in this object. I don't think. But we must be careful.' Anna looked at me.

'What? You want me to pick it up? Gross.' I looked down at the wooden thing, picked it up, and turned it over in my hands, studying the grooves. It was light. I tried to feel something from it. Nothing came.

'They sometimes coated their work with blood,' said Anna.

'Argh!' I dropped the giraffe onto the bed.

'Well, anthropologists think it was mostly during their ancient ceremonies.' Anna was perfectly thrilled.

I pulled a face at her. 'Oh, well that makes it okay, then. If you're so interested, you hold the bloody thing. No pun intended.' I grinned.

'I will.' Anna picked up the giraffe and stroked his head. I scrunched my nose up. A tiny speck of light shone from the giraffe's eyes.

'Do you see this?' said Mum.

I nodded and smiled. 'Yes, I do. Looks like Anna's made a new friend. Now if this thing detects magic like you say it does, then we might have a chance.'

Anna smiled. 'I like it.'

'I can see that,' I said.

'We have some phones calls to make,' said Mum.

'There's definitely no one home,' I said, as we watched the Armstrong's house safely from behind a bush across the street.

'The phone call was good, Connie. It worked,' said Anna, as she squeezed Mum's shoulder. 'Of course a woman like Aidah would make an appearance at an Australia Day BBQ in her new town. She'll probably run for council. There'll be plenty of people on the beach to keep her occupied. Even Mayor Tom Tate is showing up, apparently. Let's get a closer look,' Anna said as she made her way across the road without so much as a *let's go.*

We stood before the house. I'd been there three times today, once in a vision, once on my own (*what an insane thing to do*), and now. If Megan was missing, she was either here, or long gone. The thought of the little girl from my vision came back to me. She started whistling through her teeth again.

'We can climb the fence over here.' I led them to the spot. Mum needed a little boost over and she landed on the grass just as I had – with a thud, and a sore behind.

'We're looking for anything out of the ordinary. If this woman has Megan, I feel like it will be revealed to us,' said Anna as we edged along the side of the house with me in the lead.

'I'm sorry, Anna.' I stopped and looked at her. 'She *has* Megan. Or she had her. It's already been revealed. Now we just have to find out if we're too late.'

Anna's face dropped. She nodded. 'You're right, Modesta. You're right. Just wishful thinking, I s'pose.'

'Focussing,' Mum said.

We got to the yard where Aidah had been

sunbathing earlier that day. 'How are we getting in?' Mum asked.

I scanned the back of the house. On an inkling, I walked over to the back door mat, lifted it, and sure enough, there was a key.

'Hmmmm. Not very safe,' Mum muttered.

'She's a witch, Mum. She's not scared of us.' I unlocked the sliding door. 'In fact, I'm sure she's delighted by intruders. Straight into the spider's web, or lion's den, or whatever they say.'

'True,' said Anna. 'Be on guard.'

We were in. Anna grabbed my hand gently, and pulled herself forward. 'Let me lead, Mouse. Stay close,' she whispered.

The dimly lit rooms revealed nothing but ordinary, albeit eccentric furniture and trinkets. I could smell chlorine as if someone had left swimming clothes out, and all we heard was the soft tick-tock of the grandfather clock in the hallway and our feet shuffling over tiles and carpet.

Down the hall, the giraffe lit up. A yellow glowed from its eyes. Anna stopped by a door. We stared at each other. 'Could it be Megan inside?' I said.

'It feels like some kind of protection spell,' Anna whispered. 'What do you feel, Mouse?'

I closed my eyes. I felt it, too. 'Yep, I think so. But why would Aidah want to protect Megan? Shouldn't it be more like a barrier spell? This feels positive. As if Aidah is trying to protect a loved one.'

Anna nodded. Mum frowned. I pushed the door open.

We entered a bedroom with books lining an entire wall on the left, and on the right, the shelves reached the ceiling and were covered in toys. Action figures mostly, still in their boxes. There was Superman, Alien, a collection of *Walking Dead* dolls, and a large arm sticking out with *The Flight of the Navigator* alien glaring back. It moved, and we all jumped. Mum put a hand on her heart. 'S'okay,' she said. I ran my hand over a beautiful old typewriter in the corner. Hamish had been writing something that looked like a short story. He had given himself the penname, George Charles Devol, Jr.

The room smelled like lollies and aftershave. 'This is Hamish's room,' I said.

'It definitely has the feel of a young man,' said Anna.

'This Hamish,' Mum started. 'He seems nice.'

Anna and I frowned. 'You feel something?' I asked.

'No. A boy who is reading all these books is a good boy. Looking here, he has the *Bible*.' Mum pulled the book off the shelf, as if she'd sniffed it out the moment she entered.

'Mum, you can't believe that anyone who reads the Bible is good,' I said.

Mum furrowed her brow. 'He a good boy. I know it. Why else his mother have a protection spell on his room? She know he a good boy.'

'It doesn't make sense to me,' I replied. 'Why would Hamish need that kind of protection in his own home with *her* around?'

Mum stared at me like I was buffoon. 'Modesta, this spell is not for outsiders.'

Anna folded her arms. 'What do you mean, Connie?'

'This is protection spell she does to save Hamish from herself.' Mum nodded as she fingered through the *Bible*.

Anna looked at me and winked. It made sense. After all, he *was* her son. 'Clever, Mum. Very clever.' Anna was rifling through his stuff now. 'Anna? What are you looking for?'

'The giraffe glowed when I stood here.' She pulled out a bound black notebook from Hamish's drawer. 'This is important. It has to mean something.' She unwound the string at the opening and sat on Hamish's bed.

'Let's not get too comfy, eh?' I said. My arms prickled.

'Yes, Mouse. I'm sure they won't be back for at least another hour,' said Anna. She was probably right. We sat beside her.

'What you see?' said Mum, peering over Anna's shoulder.

'Lots of pictures, some art, and notes. Like a visual journal. You see?'

'Like telling the stories through the pictures? He is talent in the art,' said Mum as she pointed to some of his sketches. They were mostly natural landscapes.

'Mum, stop.' I shook my head. 'He's the bad guy. I'm sure of it.'

Anna turned the pages. 'It looks like most of the photos are just Hamish and Aidah.' Aidah stood smiling, with clear skin and bright eyes. One particular photo caught my attention. She kissed a sevenish-year-old Hamish on the cheek as they stood on the beach. 'Look at this,' I said.

'Oh, adorable.' Mum smiled.

'No it isn't.' I frowned at her, 'Mum, stop that. Hamish probably has a *Bible* to make himself look innocent to those he chokes to death in their sleep. Anyway, the point is, *really* look at the photo. What do you see?'

Mum and Anna cocked their heads sideways in perfect unison. After a while, Anna clicked her tongue. 'Look at Aidah's swimmers.'

I nodded. 'Norma Jean swimmers,' I said. 'The pointy boobs, the high waist. It's classic 40s and 50s era swimwear.'

'Maybe this not them? Maybe this is relatives,' Mum said.

'No,' said Anna. 'No, this is them. Look.'

'How old *are* they, then?' I said.

'Old.' Anna nodded. 'Really, bloody old.'

'This is not a family of Sacmis,' Mum whispered.

'What do you mean?' I glanced over at her.

'This *is* Sacmis.' Mum bit her bottom lip. We studied the photo in silence. Anna turned a few more pages. As she turned, it seemed time turned back with her, and the photos spanned centuries. The same woman and child stared back. Every now and then there would be another child with swollen eyes and an unfamiliar face. Maybe they were the Megans, and the Sonnys of the world – those who were destined to shake hands with a hell-hag who liked to devour the souls of little children.

'They've been together for a long time,' I said as I stood. I walked over and ran my hand across Hamish's 'toys,' while Mum and Anna continued looking at the journal. It was strange that Hamish should collect anything at all. It was like finding out Jack the Ripper had a toy poodle collection. *Creepy.* I moved over to study his books. Bryce Courtenay, George Orwell, even Martin and Rowling sat on his shelf next to a little HP Lovecraft, and Dostoyevsky. I ran my finger along the hardcover version of *The Philosopher's Stone.* My fingers tingled. I opened the book and leafed through the pages. At the back of the book, there was handwriting scrawled across the last few, empty pages.

Contact Spells

Jasmine, Rose, oil, candles, mirror.
"In quiet dreams I come. You see the truth.
Things can't be undone. But see the way.
I await your saving grace."

'What is that?' Anna said in my ear. I jumped and dropped the book.

'Damn, Anna,' I whispered harshly.

'Oh, sorry, kiddo. Shouldn't sneak up on you like that.'

I picked up *The Philosopher's Stone* and went to the back. 'Look at this. It was Hamish.'

'What was Hamish?' Mum came over to take a look. I held up the page.

'He writes neat for a boy,' said Anna.

'Well, he's had like a thousand years of practise. Anyway, he's the doofus who sent a message of Aidah through my mirror. The one who didn't know what he was doing. He meant to send a message it seems, but he didn't specify *what* in this spell here. He just wanted someone to see the truth. That someone ended up being me.'

Anna shook her head. 'Why didn't he just say so when you saw him the other day?'

'Something about not being able to speak aloud,' I whispered.

'Look at these symbols.' Anna pointed.

'All I know is the ankh,' I said.

'You see this one at the top. I drew this the other day at the school, Mouse. It's a symbol to protect the children.'

'You see,' said Mum. 'He a good boy. I tell you this.'

'Anna,' I said. 'Look at the upside down triangle around the ankh. It's the symbol for water.'

She nodded. 'So it is. The symbol for water and

the symbol for life. Looks like he was trying to direct his message.'

'To me?'

'To someone powerful, and like his mother. Sorry, kiddo, but like attracts like. Your aunty had the same problem.'

'What problem *exactly*?'

'We need to keep looking for Megan,' Anna said, and it snapped me out of it. She was right – enough stuffing around. We returned both of the books and we walked back into the hall.

We spread out and scoured every corner, every cupboard, every wall. There was nothing.

'She's not here,' said Anna, as we stood in the living room. The giraffe in her hand did nothing but look ugly.

'Maybe we too late. I'm sorry, Modesta.' Mum put a hand on my shoulder.

Then, I heard it…

'*Ssssss sssss, sssss sssss, sssss sssss, sssssssssss.*' Twinkle, twinkle, little star.

It wasn't Megan, but it was *someone*. 'Can you hear that?' I said. Mum and Anna shook their heads. It was coming from nearby. I leaned over toward Anna and put my ear closer to her. It was the giraffe. 'Give me that thing, will you?'

'Sure.' Anna passed me the giraffe. It felt hot in my hand. I turned in one direction and the sound grew soft. I turned in the other and it was louder.

'This way,' I said. *Twinkle Twinkle* led me all the

way to the backyard. Somewhere we had yet to look. The swimming pool and BBQ area took up most of the space so it was difficult to see that there was an entire backyard behind it. We made our way down into the yard and the giraffe grew so loud, I was afraid the neighbours would hear, but not even Anna flinched. They heard nothing.

A dome stood just a little higher than me. A fire pit sat at the entrance. Large stones surrounded it. 'It's a sweat lodge,' said Anna.

'A what?' Mum whispered.

'It's a place for sacred healing,' I said.

'The fact she has this here ... my blood boils.' Anna gritted her teeth.

'Now's not the time for anger.' I repeated something Cat would say. I'm sure it stung, but I meant it.

'Stay here,' I said. Mum and Anna immediately latched onto me. 'I mean it.' It wasn't quite me who spoke. I felt like the object in my hand grew so light it might disappear. 'Stay here,' I said again and this time, they listened. I couldn't see their faces in the dark, but I felt their fear. 'I'm not afraid,' I said. 'But guard this door all the same.'

I stood at the entry to the sweat lodge. *Twinkle Twinkle* had stopped but I could hear a whistling sound and fire crackling. A fire burned in my throat. The heat was almost too much. I paused. My chest was tight. I felt like I had in the visita earlier today. 'No!' I cried out. This time, I was aware it was a trick of the mind. I wasn't choking, not really. It was so hard to move, but I thought of Sonny, and I pushed past the threshold.

Material brushed my face and body. Skin and fur. Then, something wet.

Inside it was dark. Empty. I walked over the earth. Rocks were piled in the centre where the fire would go. I touched the walls. The giraffe in my hand lit up. My mouth opened. The whistling sound got louder. '*Muéstrame*,' I whispered. *Someone* whispered. 'Catalina?' I said. '*Muéstrame*,' I repeated. *Show me. Show me.*

Light filtered from an unseen source above me. A soft mist descended. The stones in the centre were replaced with a little girl on the dirt. I walked over to her. She didn't seem to be breathing.

I jumped as she opened her eyes. She didn't move a muscle, but she was alive. Megan gazed up at me, then shut her eyes again, as if she were too tired to move.

'It's okay,' I said. 'I'm here to help you.' I moved toward her. When Megan sat up I saw the wreck she was. Her eyes were swollen from tears, her hair matted with dirt, her cheeks sunken as if she'd been starved. She'd been here a day and looked half dead. I imagined that snaky tongue sucking out her essence.

'Come with me, sweetie.'

'I can't move,' she said. She cried out in pain.

'Don't speak, sweetie. I'll help you,' I said. She was surrounded by spells I couldn't even imagine existed, let alone fight off. I touched her and pulled my hand away. She was boiling hot.

Why hadn't I sent Anna in instead of me? She was the magic one. But I knew I'd never get her past that threshold. She'd never believe the burning was in her mind –whereas I *knew* it wasn't real. She'd be stuck there, in the space between, for Aidah, like a fisherman pulling his net into the boat. No, it had to be me.

Then ... the smell of lilac. It filled my nose. It was so lovely I could bathe in it.

The sweetest sound I'd heard in forever filled my ears. Jon Bon Jovi crooned from the ether.

Cat.

Somehow, Cat was here with me. Somehow she got through whatever thing it was holding her back, and she was with me now. Maybe she was away not only because she didn't want to be sensed by Aidah, but because she was conserving her power for something. Maybe for this.

I placed my giraffe beside Megan. My hands moved and my mouth opened – all on their own.

'Invoco la luz en mi corazón.'

I raised my hands up higher.

'Invoco la luz en mi corazón!'

It felt so natural. I sang it.

The lodge lit up. I swung my hands around and danced and sang. My body was light, and my hair was standing up on my head. A smile spread across my face. It was so wide my cheeks hurt.

Megan sucked in air as if she'd been underwater too long. I stopped and I watched her. I watched her eyes go from blank and zombie-like, to little-girl sparkling. Her cheeks filled and flushed pink. Her hair fell softly around her shoulders, and she stood.

My hair and hands both fell back to their natural places. I felt the blood in my cheeks. 'Megan,' I breathed. 'I am here to take you home.'

She ran to me, and threw her little arms around my waist. 'Thank you, lady,' she said.

'Come with me, sweetie.' I held out my hand and she took it. 'We have to get out of here ... quick.'

Anna and Mum stood frozen at the entry and though they'd been trying to peer in must've seen and heard nothing.

'Modesta!' Mum embraced me.

'Shhhh, Mamá. Time to go.'

Anna took Megan's other hand. The little girl looked up at her. 'Principal Kirk?' she squeaked. Anna nodded. We rushed to the safety of her Ford Fiesta up the road. We didn't stop until we were home.

CHAPTER 10

'**I want to go home**, pleasssse,' Megan said for the hundredth time, the little gap in her teeth exaggerating her lisp – she was a brunette Cindy Brady with an Australian accent. 'Is Principal Kirk mad at me for running away?'

'No, no, no! Anna is proud of you, little one. And you going home very soon, honey,' said Mum. 'You mummy and daddy are on the way.' She pushed the plate of food closer to Megan. 'Please eat a little.' Megan nodded and spooned some mashed potato into her mouth.

'She remembers nothing,' Anna whispered to me. 'It's surely something Aidah does to them.' We stood in the kitchen and stole glimpses at Megan through the doorway.

'I'd prefer it that way if I were her. It's for the best, Anna,' I said. 'I've seen what's underneath *that* hood. Besides, even if Megan remembered the story, Aidah would never be convicted. She's too clever. Plus the whole deal where she makes you think she's nice as pie on Sunday.' I shook my head. 'You should've seen Megan when I first did. She was half dead, Anna. Aidah has no regard for human life. That poor little girl. I think she might've been dead.' I folded my arms.

'What do you mean?' Anna breathed.

'When I first saw her, I could've sworn she wasn't breathing. When I said the spell, she gasped for air.'

Anna stared at me. 'I thought all you needed was a spell to reveal her.'

'At first. Then when I saw her, she couldn't move from her spot. She looked awful. Just awful.'

'Why didn't you tell me?'

'I haven't exactly had time to give a full recount, We've been busy making up *another* story. Besides, she would've overheard. By the way, Megsy, I think you were pretty much dead, but don't stress, Aunty Mouse is magic,' I huffed.

'Sorry, kiddo. I know. I'm just a little stressed, too.'

'No, I'm sorry,' I said. 'I didn't mean to snap.' Anna moved over to boil the kettle, and pulled out some teacups. 'The spell was all Spanish. I memorised the words. Invoco la luz en mi corazón.'

Anna stared at me again. Then she nodded. 'That's Cat's spell. She was with you.'

I smiled. 'I know.' Tears welled in my eyes.

Anna nodded. 'It's such a clever spell. She made a long time ago. It means *I invoke the light in my heart.*'

'As soon as I said it, Megan was free. She breathed again. She changed back to her normal self,' I whispered.

'She developed it from the ancient adage, 'as above so below…''

'…as within, so without,'' I breathed. 'It makes perfect sense.'

Anna smiled. 'Bringing the light within means sending the light without.'

'I'm pretty positive Cat brought her back to life tonight,' I said as I pulled out some cinnamon tea. 'Or at least, back from the edge.'

'You did, Modesta. You and Cat together. Do you think … ?' Anna paused.

'What?'

Anna stormed out into the dining room. 'Megan, before your mum comes, I want to make sure you've got all your belongings.' Anna moved over to her. 'Can you check for me, sweetie?' Anna bobbed down to be at her side.

Megan trusted her Principal. She nodded and looked at herself. The five-year-old looked a little uncertain, at first, but then she pulled out some items from her pocket. There was a dirty tissue, a little sand, and a black object I couldn't really see.

'That'sss not mine,' she said.

'Oh, thanks, sweetheart. That one belongs to me.' Anna took the object and handed it to me. It was a black ankh. *The resurrection ankh.* The one just like future Sonny's. I stared at it for a long time.

'What is it?' said Mum as she moved over to see the pendant. She studied it, then looked at the one around my neck. She bit her bottom lip.

Red and blue lights flashed through the window. I pocketed the pendant, and moved over to open the front door. Megan's Mum, Rachael, came through first, then her father. They embraced their daughter through sobs.

'Mummy, Daddy! I'm sssorwy.'

'Ssshhh. It's all right, darling.' Rachael Small kissed her daughter's hand. She looked like ten miles of bad road.

Her husband wasn't much better. He lifted Megan up to carry her. 'Thank you, Miss Castro. Thank you, Principal Kirk,' he said. It wasn't often I heard people call Anna that. I often saw people hug her, though, and this is just what Rachael did.

'Modesta Castro?' A dark-skinned policeman with a thin moustache stood in our doorway. A female stood a few steps down, leaning on the rail with her police hat tilted sideways. She was blonde and wore too much lipstick for an officer on duty.

'Yes.' I stood back. I was in my 'comfies' and this consisted of Alice in Wonderland pyjama bottoms, a skull and cross bones hoodies, and white pom pom slippers. I had to look the part.

'We'd like to ask you a few questions.'

'Yep, sure. Mind if my mum and Anna, ahhh Principal Kirk, listen in? They were here when it all happened.'

The dark gentlemen nodded. 'I'm Inspector Russell Clark and this is Constable Leonie Grace.' He held out a hand and shook mine firmly. Leonie didn't have the same manners. I let them step through the door and into the living room with the rest of us. Inspector Clark shook hands with Mum and Anna. 'Mr and Mrs Small would like to take Megan home immediately, as I'm sure you understand. I've told them your story and they're very grateful.'

Rachael nodded through tears. 'I don't know how to thank you again.' I almost welled up with her.

'It's all right,' I said. 'All I did was spot her through the window. It looked odd to see a little girl wandering the street so late at night. We went outside, brought her in, and that's when Anna realised she was Megan.'

'We called you straight away,' Anna said to Inspector Clark and Constable Grace, who looked *thrilled* to be here as she folded her arms.

'You're going to be Megan's teacher, we hear?' Mr Small said as he shook my hand.

'Yes. I'll see her in class when she's ready. She doesn't seem to remember what happened to her, or where she's been. Please don't be hard on her,' I said. 'Take her to talk to somebody.'

'We will,' said Rachael. 'Megan, baby, are you

ready to go home now?' Megan nodded. 'Goodbye.'

Anna nodded. 'See you soon.'

The Smalls left. Megan was covered in protection spells since Anna got to her, but I was still terrified to let her go.

We escorted Clark and Grace to the dining room table, and we squeezed around it. 'Well, I'm obviously not under arrest.' I smiled. Neither of my guests returned it. Mum glared at me.

'Not yet,' said Grace. Sarcasm was the order of the day, apparently. She reminded me of Traci Lord's character in the *Tommyknockers*. I was waiting for her to pucker her lips at me and reapply her red lipstick.

We went over our story, each of us playing our parts, and before long Clark and Grace seemed satisfied enough to leave us. They gave us contact numbers and a threat that they could return. They also mentioned the media might try to talk to us, but we had no obligations.

We were left sitting around the table with remnants of our tea. 'Do you think she'll be all right?' I said. 'Megan, I mean.'

'I don't know.' Anna rubbed her forehead. 'I hope so.' She seemed a little defeated.

'We'll find a way to stop this,' I said. 'I know it.'

She nodded. 'I need to lie down for a while.'

'Oh, me, also,' said Mum. 'You okay for a while?' She rubbed my shoulder as they headed off to bed.

'Yeah, I need to make a call. Goodnight.' It was getting closer to nine and I needed to call Trent.

It was still okay to call the home phone and catch Carey first, as I'd promised.

I went to my bedroom and closed the door. Carey answered on the second ring. 'Mouse! Rick said you'd call. I feel like we haven't seen you in forever. How's it all going?'

'Hi Carey, yeah, sorry. It's been pretty hectic with uni.' I tried to sound cheery.

'You know, I have a great big chook in the freezer downstairs ready to come out for roasting. It has your name on it, Mouse. How about tomorrow night?'

'I'll be there straight after work,' I said. I'd be with Sonny all day at school tomorrow but it wouldn't hurt for me to work some magic at the Albright's house as well. I'd use the glyph drawings Anna did at the school. This whole being *normal* thing was starting to sound tiring. Maybe I should just turn into a hermit and move to the mountains where visitas and long-tongued, soul-sucking witches wouldn't bother me.

Or I wished I could be someone like Carey Albright. She and Rick had been together since they were teenagers. First loves. They had surfed together just like Trent and I, and were just as in love as when I'd first met them twelve years ago. 'I'll get Trent for you.' I realised Carey had been waffling on and I hadn't heard a word.

'Okay, see you tomorrow.'

I only waited a few seconds before Trent spoke. 'Mouse.' His voice was warm and familiar.

'How's Sonny?' I said.

'Fine. Just normal,' he whispered. 'He's a bit suspicious as to why I won't leave him alone.' Trent chuckled.

I shifted on the bed. 'Understandable. Look, I'm going to see him in class tomorrow. Then, I'll be there tomorrow night for dinner, all right? He'll be in sight. I want to do some spells. You can help me.'

'Yep. Righto. I'm your apprentice. Whatever it takes.' He was serious. 'Mouse, thank you for everything. Listen, I heard about that Megan girl on Facebook. Mum and Dad haven't seen it yet. She's in Sonny's class. Is she missing instead of Sonny? Does this stuff work like that?'

'I don't know, Trent. But you don't have to worry about that anymore. She's safe.' I still felt so terrible for not being able to tell Trent about Aidah and Hamish, but I knew exactly what he'd do if he found out.

'Really? Anything I can do?'

I laughed. 'Just talking to you makes it easier. All you need to know is everything is all right for now.'

'Mouse, when you need me, you let me know. I mean it.' He used his firm voice.

'I will,' I said. 'Promise.' I didn't need him, just yet.

I'd slept better than I thought I would, and I now sat in my neatly-ironed clothes across from Anna at her desk. She was Principal Kirk today, and I was Miss Castro. The room smelled of incense and the eye of horus hung on the wall above Anna, next to her many awards and certificates. This would've seemed strange for a new person, but those who knew Anna knew she believed in all the religions, and the symbols, myths and legends that went along with them. She wasn't a non-denominational Principal, she was *all*-denominational.

'Relax as much as possible, Modesta. We're here with as many kids as we can manage at the moment. Be aware of the signs. If Aidah is nearby, I'm sure we'll know.'

I nodded, but there was a knot in my throat. My stomach wouldn't settle. I was so nervous it was hard to breathe. 'I don't feel right.' I brushed my hair down that kept frizzing up due to the imminent summer storm outside. At least my hair was a good rain-detector.

There was a knock at the door and I jumped. Anna glared at me as if to say, *chill out, you nutcase.* Carla, one of the office ladies, entered and said, 'There's a parent here to see you.'

'And it begins. Send them in. I'll speak to you soon, Mouse.'

I wanted to leave with Carla, but I felt glued to my chair. I couldn't stand. Anna stared at me again. When she looked up, she understood.

'Thank you for seeing me.' Aidah walked in like a breeze – fresh and sweet. Her hair was neat and pulled back, her make-up light, her clothes loose and flowing. This was Aidah – pretty, warm, inviting

– like one of those spiders who mimics the smell of an ant before it devours them. We were the ants.

Aidah's eyes locked onto the eye of horus for just a little too long. 'I'm Aidah Armstrong.'

'Carla said you were a parent.' Anna sat and clasped her hands together on the desk and raised her eyebrows.

'Oh, no, did she? I'm not. My Hamish is finished his schooling. I'm actually here to offer my services as a community helper. My forte is reading, but...' she looked at me. 'Have I caught you at a bad time?' Aidah smiled. Anna glared at her, and Aidah seemed surprised we weren't warm and melting like buttered-up toast by now. 'May I take a seat?'

'Well, I'd offer you tea, but the bell is about to go, and we have to start the day. Modesta here is about to begin her internship.'

Aidah sat anyway. That perfect smile faded fast when her eyes fell upon my special necklace. She swallowed and looked up into my eyes. She really hadn't known who we were until now. Maybe she'd had some kind of inkling and wanted to check us out. Maybe the spells outside had actually drawn her in instead of keeping her away. Well, it was too late now – might as well exert some power. 'Oh, you like my necklace? Beautiful, aren't they?' I said with a grin. I'd added Megan's to the chain this morning.

Anna bit her lip.

'Lovely,' said Aidah. 'Where on *earth* did you procure them?'

'Oh, it was easy enough. Anna and I are pretty resourceful,' I replied.

Anna shuffled in her seat. 'In fact, we collect them,' she said – starting to catch onto the dangerous game. 'If you happen to see any more around, please let us know. We'll take them off your hands.'

Aidah laughed. It sounded like bells. She was amused. 'I'm a jewellery collector, too,' she said. 'What a coincidence. I've travelled far and wide and have gathered many beautiful pieces in my time. In fact, I have some *thousands* of years old.'

'You do? Wow.' Anna was enjoying herself a little too much now. Talk about stirring up a hornet's nest.

What was I thinking starting this? Maybe we could take the focus off the kids and put it on us. 'Anna and I have only just started our collection. But we're extremely dedicated to the cause. In fact, so much so, it will take up our every waking moment. We won't let much get in our way, will we Anna?' I smiled and cocked my head. I felt sick to the stomach with fear, but hid it well. I held my hands under the table so Aidah wouldn't see them shaking.

'Unfortunately, many of my possessions come from deceased estates.' Aidah pouted. 'But I try not to let that bother me.'

'Well, that is quite sad,' said Anna. 'Let's hope nothing happens around *here*. We don't like that kind of thing.'

'You can't help nature.' Aidah rubbed a spot on Anna's desk. 'Death is everywhere you go, I'm afraid.'

'Not in my school.' Anna stood. This was going south *fast*.

The bell rang. 'Well,' said Aidah. 'I'd better let you get on with your day.' She stood. 'Good-bye, ladies.' She was almost though the door.

Anna spoke through gritted teeth. 'Keep your grubby, goddamned hands off my kids, or I'll skin you alive.'

Aidah turned and gave a half smile. 'Well,' she said. 'This place just got a whole lot more interesting.' She let the door slam behind her.

Anna and I let ourselves breathe again. Moments later we were cackling with nervous laughter. 'What did we just do?' I said.

'Exactly what Cat would've done. We let her know we exist.'

'I'm not sure that was such a good idea.' I shook my head. I was still giddy. 'She knows we took Megan, too. She knows we got through her barricade.'

Anna nodded. 'She thinks she knows how powerful YOU are. And you know what, Miss Modesta Castro, I don't think even you or I have established the magnitude of you just yet. I think you've got something in you the likes of which she's never seen. Did you catch the look on her face when she saw those ankh? I bet it's been a long time since she was challenged like that.'

'That's the thing. She's had practise. We haven't,' I said.

'Don't underestimate yourself. Besides, Aidah

can't work magic inside these gates, or she would've done something just now. No witch, no matter how old and restrained, could've stopped herself. She would've attacked if she could.' Anna folded her arms. 'Now get to class before the second bell rings.'

As I made my way to class, I couldn't make up my mind. Did I want to be that powerful? I supposed I no longer had a choice.

CHAPTER 11

WHEN I ENTERED the classroom I'd be spending the next ten week in, the children sat in desks of four, fidgeting like children do.

The teacher, Ms Lawson, was letting the students settle in their new places for the term. She was chatting with a parent so could only offer me a quick nod.

'Hi,' Megan smiled at me from a desk below.

'Well, good morning. I'm surprised to see you back so soon,' I said.

'I didn't want to misss the first day back,' she said with her lisp.

'You must have a special teacher,' I said. Megan nodded with that toothless grin.

'Mouse!' Sonny ran over and hugged me.

'It's Miss Castro today.' I held him tight, and ruffled his lemon hair.

'I have to go and get my desk ready. I'll see you soon. Will you come and see me at my desk?' he said.

'Every day.' I grinned. Sonny ran off and Megan motioned for me to bend down. I complied. She whispered to me. 'They have isse cweam and fizzy dwinksss in heaven.'

My chest tightened. 'Do they?'

'Miss Castro.' Ms Lawson was tall and lean, and looked like she ran marathons. Her magnolia-print dress fell over her firm skin, and she was neither young nor old. Perhaps she was a rower, with her strong arms and sun-kissed brow.

'Lovely to meet you again, Ms Lawson.' I stood and extended a hand. I heard Megan whistling through the gaps in her teeth to the tune of *Twinkle Twinkle*. There was a tingle down my spine. *They have isse cweam and fizzy dwinksss in heaven.*

Ms Lawson shook my hand and smiled at me with straight white teeth. 'Sorry I didn't get to you sooner. I had a parent to talk to. Thank you for looking after your new teacher, Megan.' Megan beamed. Ms Lawson lowered her voice as she guided me to the front of the room. 'I heard about what happened to Megan over the weekend. Thank goodness for you...' She didn't seem to know what else to say.

Ms Lawson showed me where to put my belongings and started her class with the roll call.

The morning didn't drag as I suspected it would, and it was because of Ms Lawson. She knelt to reach the children at their desks for consultations. She was a mover, a teacher who went around and gave each student individual attention. This was a difficult thing to do all the time, but a moving teacher knew her students. She knew where they were at, in every subject, and exactly where they needed to go.

'Ms Lawson, I need to pee.'

'Hand down, Ronny, you just went to the toilet, and we say urinate.'

I supressed a smile. I noticed she'd kicked off her shoes and was wandering the classroom barefooted. She was so much like me, and to impress your prac teacher you had to morph into them, in a sense. I knew exactly why Anna had put me here.

Sonny refrained from calling me Miss Mouse. He was a perfect gentlemen. It felt good to be able to keep an eye on him.

'Miss Casstwo?' Megan said, raising her hand, even though I was standing right there.

'Yes, Megan? Can I help you with your handwriting? By the look of your letter 't's, you don't need any help.' I knelt beside her again. 'Am I going back to the tent?' She looked right through me.

I shivered. 'No, honey. You're not going back to the tent.' I put my hand on her arm. 'Principal Kirk and I will make sure of that.'

She *remembered*.

'What else do you remember, Megan?'

She looked up at me confused. 'What do you mean, Misss Castwo?'

'Never mind,' I said. 'It's all right.'

'You have one minute before morning tea, friends,' Ms Lawson said. 'I expect you to be finished with your handwriting.' She walked over to me as I stood. A knot had formed in my throat and it sat there like a fat toad. That morning replayed in my head and the thought of Aidah made me sick. *Death is everywhere you go, I'm afraid.*

'Miss Castro.' Ms Lawson placed a hand on my shoulder. 'Would you like to take a few minutes outside before the place is overrun?'

'Thank you.' Just a little fresh air would do me good.

I wandered to the back of the school where the gardens were large and wide. Grevillas, anthuriums, and bottlebrush were in bloom and the honeyeaters were in a feeding frenzy. I watched them fly about and thought of Megan and Sonny.

My eyes were drawn to a figure. A woman draped in rags who looked as if she hadn't showered in several weeks glared at me from beyond the school fence. Her hair framed her face in grotty clumps, yet she looked familiar.

Aidah. Aidah as she truly was. I saw her lick her black lips with her long tongue. Her skin was transparent. She stood at the fence as if she couldn't enter. Maybe in her natural form, she couldn't. The kids filtering into the playground couldn't see her.

My fingers tingled, and the hair on my neck stood on end as she watched me, unmoving. I had an urge to go to her. It was as if she needed my help, and my body started moving without my permission.

STAY BACK.

Cat shrieked in my head like a banshee, but my trance didn't break. My lids drooped and my arms and legs prickled. I watched Aidah call to one of the boys. He made his way to the fence. 'No!' I wanted to scream but nothing came. Aidah grasped the arm of the child. He didn't react. He just stood and looked at the woman at the fence as if all was wonderful, as if their destination was Candyland. He jumped over to her. *So much for the protection spells!*

I watched her drag the boy across the street. Then my feet listened to my brain and I gave chase. Aidah held the boy's hand now, and they rushed across the lower highway together, out of sight. I pushed on as hard as I could toward the gates.

Parents on the street watched me as we ran across the road. The people at the bus stop looked at me, confused. Aidah and the child were on the other side of the main highway, on their way to the beach. To the water. Aidah stopped and turned to look at me. It wasn't Aidah's face looking back.

It was mine.

I stepped out into the street and dodged several cars. There were horns and yelling, and extended fingers. I stepped around a white station wagon.

Aidah stopped in her tracks, and her own face

returned.

'You will not harm the child!' I screamed.

Her mouth grew impossibly wide with a wicked grin. I moved closer to them. Aidah opened her mouth and the black space became even wider. Water poured out of it, and the highway under my feet filled up like a small bucket. It was up to my knees in seconds. People in cars jumped out and waded to higher ground. Parents with panic-stricken faces screamed to unbuckle their children. The smell of the ocean wasn't so soothing now. I didn't know what to do.

The water was up to our necks in a matter of moments, and Aidah held the boy's head under. Her eyes were wild, and a deep satisfaction spread over her face. The boy thrashed about. She was killing him!

I knew I couldn't overpower her, so I did what came to me first. I dived under and shoved the ankh pendant into the boy's mouth. He gasped and spluttered and opened his eyes. He could breathe under water. Aidah let out a deafening screech. She let go of the boy as if he were on fire, and then flames surrounded me like I had jumped out of the pot and into the frying pan.. Smoke engulfed me, but I didn't suffocate. My throat didn't burn. I moved freely.

Colours became saturated and heavy shapes merged together. I was inside Aidah's living room. The place was falling apart as flames licked the ceiling and the roof came down around me. Aidah was screaming and came tearing into the room to stand before me.

The screaming stopped. Her chest heaved. '*Ojo por ojo*,' she said.

I understood. *An eye for an eye.* She grabbed me by the face and pulled me down into the flames with her. I felt the heat, but I didn't burn.

Aidah did, though.

Her face melted before me like wax down a multi-coloured candle, and her hands ran onto my arms. She melted onto me.

Hamish came though the flames. I couldn't hear his words. I understood the sadness on his face. He'd lost his mother. She'd burned to death in my arms.

Then ...

... I was back.

I was back on the sidewalk out the front of the school, looking over the road, and Aidah was gone. Hamish was gone. The flames were gone. And I was holding the boy from school far too tight. I pulled away. I'd left a horrible red mark.

'Let him go!' one of the onlookers shouted.

'That woman was taking that boy away.'

What? I looked down, and tears were streaming down his terrified face. He looked as if he'd wet himself at the sight of me. *Oh no.* What had Aidah done? What had *I* done?

A woman with purple-flowered bellbottoms shouted and pointed at me. 'Call the police. Someone grab her!'

'No, I'm a teacher here. This boy was in danger.'

'From who and from what?' said Bellbottoms. She led the distraught boy away, never taking her eyes off me.

I kept my head down, and made my way into the school gates, and straight to Anna's office. We'd just had a pissing contest with Aidah. She'd won.

'Mouse? It was Aidah, wasn't it?' I sat across from Anna again. I could hardly look up at her. My throat was hoarse. 'One minute I was in the yard for recess. The next, I was over the other side of the road holding a random boy's arm.' The tears came in sobs. I cried so hard and so suddenly I couldn't breathe. There were days of built up tension in my sobs. Anna was by my side in a heartbeat. 'It's okay. It's okay,' she whispered as she put her arms around me. Carla came in with tea for the both of us. When she saw my crying, she apologised and let herself out.

'It was my fault. I stirred Aidah up. I shouldn't have,' said Anna.

'We did the right thing,' I said, wiping some tears away. I sipped my chamomile tea. 'It *is* what Cat would've done. We needed to know if she could get to us, to the kids. Well, she can.'

Anna nodded. She sat back down across from me and I told her about the water, how I used the ankh to save the boy, and then the fire.

'*Bruja del agua,*' Anna whispered.

'What?' I breathed.

'Water Witch, Mouse. Aidah is a Water Witch.' Anna shook her head. 'So was Sacmis. I looked further into it. She was found by the Nile, bruised and battered. Remember? There are traces of her all over the place. I'll show you.' Anna opened her laptop. She turned it around so I could see as she scrolled down. There were several links and documents.

'Please, just tell me the most important part.' I was too exhausted to look at her evidence. I didn't want to put faces to the suffering. I just knew it had to stop.

'She's like you in that she uses water for power, Mouse. It's why she's here, on the coast.' Anna stood. 'Bruja del agua drowns her victims. This one, in particular, uses an ankh to resurrect them. It's why the ankh worked in your visions.' Anna was pacing the room. 'It was a vision by the way, honey. None of that actually happened, except that you took a little boy over the road. She made you see something that wasn't there. The part that concerns me was that she took over your mind so easily.'

'She made me *see*. Like Cat did for you and Mum. This is just great,' I said. I took some tissues and blew them to smithereens.

'Don't give up now, kiddo. We've got this.'

'I don't feel like it. Not even a little.'

Anna held my by the shoulders and looked into my eyes. 'Modesta Castro, have I ever let you down before?' she said.

'No, you haven't,' I said. 'There's one thing I don't get, though.'

'What's that?'

'Why would she resurrect them?'

Anna paused for a moment, then shook her head. 'I dread to wonder.'

CHAPTER 12

'MOUSE?' SONNY'S VOICE WOKE ME. A cold blue hand reached out and ran itself over my arm. It was slimy. My skin prickled where he touched it. 'Mouse?' he said. He shook me. His voice was low and gurgling, as if he had a mouth full of water, and when I looked at him – he did. It trickled down his chin. His skin was bloated and pieces of it dangled from his face like seaweed.

'Sonny.' I touched his hand, but it was goo. Bits of it stuck to me as I drew my trembling fingers away. His eyes were sorrowful. Tears welled in them. His small hand motioned for me to follow.

My poor Sonny. I'm coming.

The house was lit up with green and aqua-blue

lights, like a kiddies' disco party. I followed Sonny through the corridor, out the door and into the night. I shivered in the night air – it was so cold, even though it was supposed to be summer. Sonny kept turning back to make sure I was coming; his little legs moved faster than I would have thought possible for someone with pieces of dead flesh dropping from his swollen body with every step.

We arrived at the beach. Sonny stopped and looked down at the water, so I did, too. There was movement in the blackness. Sonny pointed at it. I wasn't sure what I was looking for, but when my eyes made it out, I didn't want to see the ghastly scene before me anymore.

Hundreds of people floated to the surface and emerged from the water. And just like Sonny, they were falling to pieces – eyeless, water-ravaged corpses, their bodies full of holes, silently came toward us with drooping skin.

I don't want to see your faces.

Sonny looked up at me, somehow aware that I was about to run for my life. With impossible strength, he clasped my hand in an iron grip and made me stay.

They surrounded us.

Some of the drowned children tugged on my shirt. Black objects pierced the septums in some of their noses. *Ankh.* Not all of them had it. Just a few.

One of the adult's skin was sagging so badly at first, I didn't recognise her. She opened her mouth. 'Modesta,' she whispered, and as she did, the small leg of a blue-ringed octopus slithered out. It was searching for me.

'Mum?' Tears streamed down the corpse's face, and mine, too. I shook my head, 'No, Mum!'

My own scream woke me.

Mum's face loomed. She was alive, and normal. I'd fallen asleep on the couch and she was bending over me.

'You okay, Modesta?'

I reached up and kissed her. 'Yeah,' I said. 'I am now. It was just a bad dream.' I sat up on the couch and Mum slid in beside me.

'They say the dream is the place where your deepest fears come true to the surface,' she said.

'I'd believe it after *that* dream.'

'You like some tea?' Mum said.

I smiled. 'Not just yet, thanks.' Anna had sent me home 'sick.' I wasn't, but I felt like I'd been hit by a truck, and that sufficed. Great impression for my first day of internship. Ms Lawson was fine with it, though, and associated it all with the shock of what happened to Megan. She was partly right. 'Mum?'

'Sí?'

'Cat died in a fire,' I said.

'Yes.' Mum nodded.

'She could make you think things. Do things, like Aidah can?'

Mum nodded again.

'Are we all the same?' I brushed some damp strands of hair from my face.

'*Sí*, Modesta. In many ways, you are the same. There is somethings your aunty, she used to say … like is attracting like. The same is wanting to be near the same, you understand?'

'Yeah. I do.'

'Catalina meet with other witches, too, you knows? Is how she lost her fingers, she tell you?'

I shook my head. 'I asked once, but I never found out the whole story.'

'A witch burned her hand.'

I frowned. 'She said it was water. '

'Yes.' Mum shuffled in her seat.

'I don't understand. *Agua* is … safe for us. I always thought fire was the enemy – the opposite element. Aidah burned in my vision today, so I was kinda hoping it was the answer to our problems.'

'Catalina wanted something that was not belong to her. She was always taking the things that were not hers.' Mum rolled her eyes. "Specially if it had the magic. So, of course, she try to steal from a witch. The witch caught her. Luckily Catalina did not die this day. But her hands was badly burned with water. She could stop her pain, but not bring back her fingers. She never steal from a witch again, I tell you now!' Mum elbowed me and I chuckled. 'The water, she say was so hot, it explodes. Right on her hand. Terrible. She laugh about it later, but not so funny at the time.'

I thought for a moment. 'I've heard of this in physics,' I said. 'Superheating. The water doesn't look hot, but it's heated so fast it explodes. Something about bubbles not forming.'

'Your aunty had to learn how to do it, of course. You knowing her, she always had to be the winner. To know *everything*. She did it, too. Catalina made water explode in the kitchen sink. I never saw anything like it. Almost killed me two times.' Mum put two fingers up to emphasise the number of impending deaths.

'You're joking, I hope. But this is genius, you realise? This superheated water was able to hurt Cat, so it could hurt Aidah as well. All I have to do is figure out how the hell she did it,' I said.

'Watching your language or I be getting soap.' Mum patted my knee. 'Well, I am not sure how to explode the water, but I can boil the kettle for tea. You sure you okay?'

I smiled at her – my sweet, sweet mother. 'I'm better now,' I said.

Just don't go near the water, Mum. There's an octopus waiting for you. Would everything haunt me now? Octopi, tongues, green pants, and frilly dresses. 'Peppermint tea for me, please.'

I made my way to the bathroom and splashed some water over my face. Then I filled the sink and stared down at it, concentrating with everything I had. I stood back, just in case it worked. I tried this superheating trick for over half an hour, but the water didn't even hit luke-warm. 'How, Cat? How do I do this?'

I wanted to talk to Anna, but she would still be at work for the next couple of hours. She'd given me a little hope when she'd dropped me off out front in her Fiesta. 'Try to remember that each time you've found yourself in trouble, Mouse, you've known exactly what to do. That's not just good luck, kiddo. You've got powers beyond belief on your side,' she'd said. 'I'm not worried. We're gonna be all right.'

I had hugged her. 'That's what I said to you last night.'

'You did,' Anna had said. 'And you were right. We're gonna figure this out. Everything we need to know will come to us.'

'Everything we need to know will come to us,' I had repeated to her. I stood up, returned to my water in the sink, and I repeated it now in the mirror. 'Everything I need to know will come to me.' I looked down at the sink. 'Come on, water, boil, you bastard!'

Nothing.

I noticed a bag sticking out from under one of the clean towels. It was the mugwort, cinnamon, and star anise Anna had given me the other night. I'd dreamed of Hamish before I'd met him. It had given me answers, then. It was worth another look. I grabbed the bag and ran a bath. 'Mum,' I called. 'I'm going back under.' It wasn't long before I was out.

The phone rang, and I answered it before the second ring. Without even a 'hello,' Trent cried, 'Mouse, Sonny's gone!'

'*What?*'

'I can't find him!' Trent shouted.

'Oh, no.' *Please no.* I rubbed my eyes. 'I'm going over there.'

'Going where?'

I hung up.

I pulled on my pants. I held onto my ankh. And I ran.

I was standing before the Armstrong house. Weeds wound their way up to the roof. Cream paint peeled like filo dough. The weatherboard was falling off in chunks. I'm not sure anyone else could see the house the way I saw it, if the way it looked was real to anyone but me. It was falling apart. Surely no one else could smell the miasma of stench that overlaid it like ground fog, or the police would've been called to check for dead bodies.

Aidah was at the window. She looked worse than ever – skeletal – like she'd been starving for months. She was the spiritual embodiment of every childhood nightmare, the thing crouching in the closet, the bogeyman hiding beneath the bed.

'Let me in,' I called. 'I know you have him, you cow.' I jumped the fence in my usual spot and thumped on the front door. Fear and adrenaline kicked my heart into overdrive and made my blood pump so loudly, I could hardly hear myself. 'Give him back. You can't have him!'

I shook the handle and it broke off in my hand.

I moved back to the window. Aidah smiled with black teeth, and the hideous smell from the decay was stronger, even though the panes of glass. She curled her mouth into an 'O' shape and sucked in a huge breath.

Then the screaming started.

The screaming of a child.

Sonny!

I smashed the broken door handle against the window, but it bounced off.

I cast about for something heavier and when I looked up again, crimson mist filled the air around Aidah, before she began to change. Her face filled out, her hair softened, and the lines around her eyes disappeared.

The house changed, too.

It repaired itself. The weeds shrank away.

And still, the screaming. Sonny's screams.

I spied a good-sized rock, snatched it up, and hammered away at the window. It finally cracked. Aidah, who had clearly cast a strengthening spell on the glass, stood unwavering. Still inhaling, and still growing younger.

Sonny, sobbing, screamed, 'Mummy, help me!'

'Don't worry, baby, Mouse is coming,' I cried. I punched a hole in the glass at last. Aidah stopped her mouth hoovering, and that's when the screams suddenly stopped.

I was too late.

The rock fell from my hand.

The new Aidah gazed at me through the hole in the window and smiled.

The rock was too slow. I gathered my strength and rammed the window with my shoulder. The whole thing shattered and Aidah laughed. She pulled me through it, needle-sharp glass shards raking my body and cutting my stomach and legs.

Her fingers clenched my wrist and burned it like five drops of acid where they dug in. Her slimy wet tongue dug into my ear and filled my head with a horrible sucking sound. It felt like she was syphoning out my soul – feeding on me without biting down— like she'd just done to my Sonny.

I grabbed my ankh. I searched for words to stop her, but nothing came. It was as if she'd drained away my thoughts and rendered me as pliable as a sparrow.

This time I'd die.

I pulled at my ear where her tongue stabbed in and out, and screamed and thrashed.

The energy was leaving my body, my life force was disappearing. I knew then and there, *this* was how she lived forever. She'd draw out my soul, and then she'd store me like an old dress in a closet for a while, then revive me, and do it all over again. An eternity of inescapable torture. I'd be one of her dead coterie. One more who walked from the water, haggard and sopping wet, with octopus arms flailing from my mouth.

Like Sonny.

Like Mum would be if I didn't stop this now.

And I knew I wouldn't. I couldn't. The strength and the will to do it were nearly gone.

'Get off her!' Hamish screamed.

Maybe I *wouldn't* die today, after all.

'Mum. STOP IT. PLEASE!'

Aidah relented. I took a breath.

CHAPTER 13

MY VISION LIT A FIRE within me. Mum had gone to work, and Anna was still at school with Sonny. I thought of calling Trent, but he would be at his internship. I had to take matters into my own hands.

I put on my shoes, locked the house, and made my way to Christine Avenue. I didn't stop for a second. I was out of breath when I jumped straight over the fence, this time landing on my feet, and I made my way around the side of the Armstrong house to what I was pretty sure was Hamish's window. There were security screens over it. At least if Aidah came to the window, I'd have a little time to high-tail it out of there before she could get to me. I knocked on the screen.

The curtains moved.

I held my breath.

Hamish peered out. I exhaled, thanking *Criede* it wasn't Aidah's ugly mug peering back. Hamish frowned, then threw open his window. 'What are you doing?' He spoke in a harsh whisper. 'If Aidah catches you here…'

'You sent me a message, Hamish,' I said. 'You're the one who invited me here. In quiet dreams I come,' I quoted his spell. 'You see the truth.'

His eyes widened. He had the security screen off in a matter of moments. Obviously, he had it at the ready. An escape route, as such. There were far worse things in his house than there were outside of it.

'Give me your arms,' he said. I thought of him in my visita trying to help me. I thought of the message he sent to find someone to help, someone to protect the children. If he wasn't on my side, I'd lost my touch, and wouldn't make it through this anyway.

I reached up. He grabbed my arms and pulled me through the window. My thighs scraped the sill. 'Ouch.'

'Sorry,' he breathed as he helped me up. He then replaced his screen, shut the window, and threw the black curtains over them.

His long dark hair was down and it fell about his face. He pushed it behind an ear, and rushed around to tidy his room. 'Did she see you?' he said.

'No. I don't think so.' I said. Coldplay crooned quietly in the background about a sky full of stars.

'This is as far as anyone's ever come.' Hamish stopped and stared at me. 'I mean. There was another, but Aidah got to him. She's weak right now … and slow. I don't know why.' He ran a hand through his hair and swallowed. 'Sorry. I talk too much when I'm nervous. No one's ever been in my room before.'

'Never?'

He shook his head. 'You don't have to worry about being quiet in here. And you can say what you want. She can't hear us. I can tell you everything. You're a witch, then?' He was out of breath too now.

'Slow down,' I laughed nervously. 'I'm still figuring out whether or not you're the bad guy.'

'What? Oh.' He raised his eyes brows, and looked down at his clothes. 'I can see how you might've thought that. Um … would you like a seat? I mean, I only have my bed. You can sit on it.'

I laughed. He was so nervous, he was shaking. 'Thanks.' I took a seat on the end. I had to calm him down a little if I wanted to get any sense out of him. 'I like your toy collection.'

'Oh? Yeah. It's kind of dumb.'

'Not really. They're cool.'

'Thanks. I've got a fair amount of time on my hands.' He smiled. He reminded me of Tate from *American Horror Story* – maybe a little crazy, dangerous, and lovable, even though he was bad for you, and probably your entire family. 'Can I sit?' He gestured to a spot next to me and I nodded. When he sat, I noticed his hands were no longer shaking.

He was calming down a little. Idle chitchat worked.

'So, Coldplay?'

He laughed. 'Yeah. I love most music. As you might've guessed from the way I dress, I like metal most. But I've been known to play a little Al Green from time to time.'

I smiled. 'Can't go wrong with the classics.'

'Classics for *you* are different than classics for *me*.'

That's right. He's old. Really old. 'How long have you been with her?' I said.

'A few lifetimes,' he said. I nodded. 'You don't seem surprised.'

'I know a little about you.' I didn't want to share too much too soon, so I stopped.

'I guess she likes having me for a son,' he said sadly.

'It must be hard.'

'Yeah. It's not a great existence,' he continued. 'I've tried to escape, in more ways than one, if you catch my drift. Let's just say, the first time I left her, it was with my own hands. Unfortunately for me, the living dead are her specialty.'

'I'm sorry to hear that,' I said, wondering if it would be too awkward to hug him. I put a hand on his shoulder instead. 'That sucks. A lot.' I tried to change the subject. 'How can you speak so freely here?'

'This is my sanctuary. I suppose since I can't invite anyone in, or tell anyone about it, she assumed I'd never have anyone inside it. It worked for a few hundred years so far. I started sending the messages about a decade ago.'

'Your spell was dodgy, you know. Aidah's image came through and cut up my hands. You have to be more specific when you send messages through spells.'

'Damn, sorry. May I see?' He touched my arm and turned it over to reveal the cuts. They were looking a little better. He ran a hand over them. My heart thrummed. *No, Mouse. Don't get a crush on someone ELSE you can't have.*

'You're a little young to be a witch, aren't you?'

I smiled. 'It started when I was nine, so yeah, probably. I'm more a seer than a witch.'

'What's the difference?'

'I see the future and can change it.'

'That's a cool trick.'

'It's a pain in the arse, actually. I don't get to choose what I see, or when I see it.'

'But you use water and can resurrect the dead. That makes you a witch,' said Hamish.

'No. I can't. I wish I could. I'd bring back a few family members if that were the case.'

'Yes,' said Hamish. 'You can.'

He moved over and pulled out The Philosopher's Stone from his shelf. I held my breath. 'You see this symbol here.' He pointed to the ankh inside the turned triangle.

Oh, the one I looked at while I was snooping through your room the other night? Sure, I see it. 'What is it?' I said.

'It represents what Aidah is. A descendant of Anubis.'

My breath caught in my throat. The image of Cat's tarot card came to mind. Anubis stood at the weighing of the souls – Anubis, keeper of the dead, Anubis, whose daughter was Kebechet, which meant *cooling water*. 'What do you mean?'

'I may not have been specific in what my message said, and I'm sorry for that.' Hamish continued. 'But I was *very* specific in who I sent it to.' He pointed to the symbols again. 'Someone who protects others.' He pointed to the top symbol, then the bottom. 'And someone who is a descendant of Anubis.' I couldn't speak. I only stared at Hamish. 'Fight fire with fire, you know? Or in this case, water with water.' Hamish chuckled until he looked up at me. 'Are you okay? You didn't know?'

'What does this mean?' I said.

'I guess it means you're bad arse, Mouse.'

I clasped my hands together. The room spinned. *Oh no. Not right now.*

A little boy sat by Aidah. She was lying statue-still. The room was dark and the walls were made from stones. 'Mama?' It was Hamish. He looked about seven years old. Aidah groaned and shivered, covered in a sheen of sweat; it was easy to see she wouldn't last without help. I walked closer to them. They made no indication that they could see me, so I inched forward. This woman was Aidah, but it wasn't. Her hair was black, her skin much fairer. She looked more like Hamish. Hamish had his long lashes even then, and his lips were small with a tiny bow. His hair was greasy, and clothes ragged. The room looked like it had been picked up 2,000 meters and dropped it was such a mess. The poor, neglected child had probably been looking after them both. It stunk of sour sweat.

'Hami,' the woman's eyes opened. She pushed some of Hamish's hair behind his ear. The little boy cried as they whispered to each other. They spoke in Spanish.

A hard knock came at the door and I jumped. Hamish ran to open it. I could hear a woman's voice. It was difficult to understand, but I managed to make out a little of the conversation.

'I can heal her ... you are safe ... The Black Death.'

Hamish let the stranger enter, and I knew it would be Sacmis. She walked in and looked straight at me. Her hair was long and luxurious. And it was copper red. Her eyes were the same colour. She walked toward me, stopping inches from my face, then sniffed the air and licked her lips. She looked older than the stories had made her out to be. Now that she was right before me I could see her fading away. She was translucent. I don't think little Hamish noticed. He was too worried about his mother, and Sacmis had dressed herself as a healer.

She grinned at me, then turned to the woman. 'Aidah,' she crooned. Sacmis carried a bag with her and removed several bottles and bandages. She asked Hamish to look away. Little Hami went to other side of the room. She told him to hide his face. He sat and put his head on his knees.

Sacmis leaned over Aidah and her long tongue licked the woman's face. Aidah passed out. Sacmis then took a knife and sliced Aidah's stomach open. She made another gash across Aidah's chest, then she breathed in deeply, then exhaled, and this time, rather than consuming the energy from Aidah, she poured herself into her. A white vapour flew from her mouth and seeped into Aidah's slashes. Aidah took a deep breath and coughed, while Sacmis lowered her weakened self to the floor until she passed out cold and thumped down on the scarred wood, like a suddenly discarded area rug.

'Mama!' Hamish cried and he ran to Aidah. She sat up in her bed. Her face was clear and bright. She smiled, ignoring Sacmis' body lying beside her on the floor. Aidah looked at me, and a hint of that evil demon showed in the curl of her lips.

I was pulled back into a vortex of blue, before I opened my eyes.

CHAPTER
14

I WOKE LYING on Hamish's bed. He was sitting beside me. 'Are you all right?' he whispered. I nodded and pulled myself up. 'What was that?'

I rubbed my eyes. It took a while before I could put words together. 'It happens sometimes. Remember how I told you I see the future?'

'Yeah.'

'Well, that wasn't it.'

He laughed.

'But it's kind of like that … when it happens. I black out for a second or two.'

'That sucks when you're driving, I bet. Can I get you anything?' I wished he would stop being so nice to me. He seemed to sense my uncomfortableness and changed the subject. 'What did you see? I mean, if you want to tell me.'

I shifted on the bed. 'One question first.'

'Fire away.'

'If you're from Spain, why the Gaelic name?'

Hamish frowned. 'It was my father's name. He travelled from Scotland and stayed at my mother's home for a few nights. She never saw him again. He never knew I existed.'

'Another sad story.'

Hamish nodded slowly. 'Yeah, sorry. I'm full of those.'

I asked Hamish about his first memory of Aidah, who wasn't Aidah. Seven-year-old Hamish had known straight away when his real mother was gone, and that the new Aidah was an imposter. I told him what I saw in my vision and he was able to connect some dots in his memory. The memory of his real mother didn't sadden him as I thought it would, yet it had happened so long ago, I supposed the pain must have subsided.

'I didn't mean to drag you into this horrible mess,' he apologised again.

I shook my head. 'It would've happened anyway.'

We spoke for a while, mostly about trivial things. It was as if Hamish just wanted to be a person, to hold normal conversations about music, art, and films. I was happy to oblige, but there was a pressing matter at hand. 'So tell me,' I finally said. 'Why did you send the message?'

'Well, every time Aidah brings a soul back, part

of it is missing. It gets to the point where they can't function properly. I've seen it and it's horrible. The more you get brought back, the less of you comes with. First it's your skills, like talking, listening, motor. Then it's whatever you were good at, art, dance, writing. Then you start to lose your identity, your personality. You become easy to influence – a minion of sorts. It's why I try to hold onto certain parts of me. My toys are a physical part of my identity, and so are my books. My music, too. But it's only a matter of time now, before I really start losing it. Some days, I lie down and the next minute it's dark. I've spent entire days as a vegetable and it's becoming more and more frequent. The more I lose of myself, the less likely it is I'll be around to keep Aidah in check. She's always been bad. But never like this.'

'What do you mean?'

'She's angry about something. Tired. Run-down. And she's taking it out on people around her – killing more than ever. I don't know what it is just yet. Aidah used to hide herself from me, pretend like she was the perfect mother. She did a pretty good job a fair amount of the time, too, if you can believe that. I didn't see or hear much of what she did. Now, I see her. The evil inside of her is coming out and is taking over this entire house.

'There've been times when I thought I could change her, help her come back to the light. There's still good inside her, Mouse, there really is. I've seen it. Then she proves me wrong. The second time

I died, it was her fault. She hasn't forgiven herself since, and I haven't been able to trust her again, as you can imagine. Now, though, she's really gone. The woman I called *mother* for such a long time has disappeared. I can't stand by anymore.' He put his head in his hands. I grabbed them, and pulled him closer. I stroked his hair and held him. His body was warm and I could feel his breath on my neck. 'You're a surprise in a world full of nothing,' he said. I knew it was odd and awkward to hold a stranger. Hamish hadn't had anyone for such a long time that I wanted to be there for him, just for a moment. I sensed it was all he really had. The dark rings around his sunken eyes told more about his exhaustion than could be expressed in words. He'd had enough now. 'I'll help you end this,' I promised.

'I had a feeling you would be coming,' he said.

'What do you mean?'

'Well, I feel peaceful. Almost like I'm ready to go now, you know? Before I was desperate to end it all. Now I'm just at ease.'

'You don't have to leave as well, do you?'

'When Aidah leaves, so will her magic. I am that magic, I guess.'

'Maybe we can find another way?' I said.

'Maybe,' he breathed. Then Hamish fell asleep in my arms. Soon he was snoring softly. I assumed it was part of his whole losing days thing. I couldn't bare to look at him lying there. I had to pull myself free. I left him a note on his typewriter.

Dear George Charles Devol, Jr.,
Inventor of the robotic arm, I'll
be back. Love, Mouse.

Trent and Sonny watched TV in our lounge room. Rick and Carey would be over later. I'd gotten my way, and we'd swapped houses for dinner tonight. Trent needed no convincing. All I'd had to tell him was tonight was the night Sonny was going to go missing if we didn't keep him by our side. He and Sonny would sleep over and I'd take Sonny to school tomorrow. 'As long as he gets to bed on time,' Carey made me promise over the phone.

'I swear Sonny will be in bed by seven. You'll be here to ensure it anyway!'

'True. We'll see you at six.'

Mum was preparing a roast in the kitchen. Anna I sat at the dining table so Trent and Sonny couldn't hear us. 'Are you sure this is going to work?' Anna asked.

'No. But I haven't been sure of much lately. How about you?'

Anna shook her head.

"Ojo por ojo,' It's what Aidah had said in one of my visions. An eye for an eye. Hamish was the son of Aidah, and Aidah was a descendant of Ptah. Sacmis lost her baby because that family threw her out when she needed them most. They owed her a child. Hamish is that child. Now he's suffering through eternity.'

'That's messed up, you know that?' Anna put a hand up to her mouth, shaking her head. 'Mouse. This is old, old magic. What we're dealing with here is… well, I've never seen anything like it.'

'You haven't even heard my plan,' I said. 'Hamish said that every time Aidah brings a soul back, part of it's missing.'

Anna looked at me sadly. 'You can't save him, Mouse.'

'Are you sure?' I said.

Anna stood. She walked around the room once, then turned to me. 'When a body dies, the soul leaves it. What happens thereafter is up to the believer. What I do know is when a soul is owed to the Gods, or Goddesses, a soul is owed. Hamish's soul was owed a long time ago, kiddo.' She said the words I hadn't wanted to hear.

The night sky suddenly opened up and the summer storm that had been building all day thrashed against the rooftop. The rain came heavy, a wall of water, and thunder boomed constantly, as if heralding the end of the world. I had to shout over the din. 'I think at this point, he just wants it all to end, anyway.'

'I don't blame him! We've only had three days of her, and I want it to end, too,' Anna said. She sat back down and leaned in. 'So, what's the plan?'

'Well, it seems that I'm not learning the trick of exploding water anytime soon.'

That's when Mum started cackling. It came from the kitchen, an almighty belly-laugh.

The thing was, it didn't sound like Mum at all.

Anna and I jumped up from the table and ran to the kitchen.

Mum's eyes had a tinge to them I didn't recognise. A subtle haze glimmered from them as she turned away. The light shone off her hair.

Copper.

'Mum?'

Anna stepped in front of me. 'Connie?'

Mum ran her finger along the lines of the kitchen bench. 'Do you like your new tapestry? The one of the kittens?' she said. But it wasn't *her* voice.

'You made that for me years ago. Of course I like it,' I said.

Anna shook her head and moved me back toward the door.

'Do you think I should make a tapestry for the Albrights, darling? I do believe they need something cheerful to remind them that life is peachy. Even after tragedy. We really must focus on them, rather than ourselves, don't you agree?'

'Connie? Why are you speaking like that?' Anna said.

'Speaking like what, darling? I'm afraid I'm not entirely sure what you're talking about.' Mum turned and stared at us. She chuckled. Her false, cheery disposition and blank eyes...

Anna and I recoiled.

'I'll fix you some sandwiches to take with you to school tomorrow. I'll make some cucumber sandwiches for the funeral.'

'What funeral, Connie?' We were at the door now, and Trent had realised something was going on. The wind howled and shook the windows.

Trent jogged in and stood behind me. 'Take Sonny to the main bathroom,' I said. 'Lock the door. Give him a shower or something so he doesn't get scared.' Trent nodded. He trusted me wholeheartedly and I could've kissed him for it.

'Sonny Albright, what a good little boy. He'll come to me no matter you do. He'll come to me because he is *miiiiine*. Megan, too. They'll always be mine, and they'll always come.' Mum turned around, her mouth grew wider by the second. It was bleeding in the corners. The cracks got larger. Her eyes were red, and her skin grey.

'No.' I ran and held onto her. 'Mum!' I screamed. Anna pulled me back. 'No, Anna. Please hold her!'

Anna stared at me for a moment or two, then realised what I was doing. She threw her arms around both of us. 'Connie Castro, you fight this!' We held on tight.

'Mum. Come back.'

'Get off me.' Arms thrashed and Anna and I went flying across the room. I crashed into a cupboard and hit my head hard. Aidah's voice came through like a roaring dragon – deep, dark, and low. 'You die now, Mousey Mouse.' The thing that was Mum, that was Aidah, came at me. It picked me up off the lino and flung me across the room like dirty clothes on a bedroom floor. I landed with a thud. My ribs ached. My right arm felt dead. I looked up to see small feet by my face.

'Sonny. Get out of here. Go back to Trent!'

He stood so still. He was in his red undies. Every fibre of my being screamed as I pulled myself up. 'Anna? Take Sonny away.' She was out cold.

Trent came in to stand beside him. He looked at Sonny terrified, and tried to pull him away. His brother was stuck to the spot. 'Sonny. Run!'

Aidah came toward him and stopped. She sniffed the air. Sonny cocked his head. His little eyes scanned Aidah up and down, then they moved. They moved in a way I've never seen eyes move before. Up, down, side, to side: so fast I could barely identify the directions.

'Argh!' Aidah rushed toward him again and then it seemed she was thrown backwards and hit the floor. The body of my mother lie still.

'Mum!' I ran to her. She gasped for air. Her eyes widened and a knowing look spread over her face. Her hand flew to her chest. 'I sorry. I so sorry!' She sucked air into her lungs. 'What happened? What am I doing?'

I searched her eyes. They were Connie Castro's now. Just like that, Aidah was gone.

I threw my arms around my mother. 'It's okay. It's over, Mum.' She sat up and rubbed her head where she'd hit it on the lino. I put a hand up to my ribs to make sure they weren't broken. They were sore, but nothing too serious.

Anna moved over and put her hand on my shoulder. 'What just happened?'

'Sonny.' I turned around and Trent was hugging his little brother. 'Sonny stopped her.' We all stood up and waited for Trent and Sonny to finish their embrace.

'I'll have my shower now.' Sonny said.

Trent shook his head. 'Yeah, in a minute, matie. First you need to tell us what you just did to the bad lady.'

'I don't know. She wasn't Connie, that lady.'

I nodded and moved over to kneel by him. 'That's right. You knew she wasn't my mum.'

'I told her to leave,' he whispered.

'How did you do that, Sonny?'

'With my head. She was angry. She wanted to hurt everybody.'

The realisation hit me. Sonny Albright. He wasn't just someone I had to protect for the greater good. He was a *brilliant*, powerful-beyond-words, someone I had to protect. No wonder Aidah wanted him. His essence would probably keep her alive indefinitely.

Anna came to the same conclusion. 'We have something on our hands bigger than all of us.' She pulled me to my feet. 'Aidah's probably a little shocked after what just happened. We strike now.'

I nodded.

'I'll have my shower now,' repeated Sonny. Trent laughed nervously. 'Come on, buddy.' He ushered his brother to the bathroom.

The home phone rang. Mum went to answer it, but Anna stopped her, told her to sit on the couch for a minute, and answered it herself.

I couldn't hear every word Anna said, but I saw her face drop. She hung up the phone, and approached me. She spoke in a whisper. 'The police just called. Rick and Carey Albright were in an accident.'

'Are they okay?' I whispered.

Anna shook her head.

CHAPTER 15

I HAD HELD TRENT TIGHT for so long my arms ached. His body had heaved with each sob. His eyes had remained hidden on his saturated sleeve. *I didn't see it coming.*

After Trent had calmed down, I'd told him everything. There was no way I'd ever be able to take back what had happened tonight. There was no way I could have saved Rick and Carey Albright, because they hadn't come to me in a visita. They hadn't come to me with blue, rotting flesh from the water, or shown me a car crash in the rain. I'd seen nothing. I tried to push them from my mind – the pain was too unbearable right now, and we had things to do. Now

I knew what Cat had felt like when the thought of Nan and Pop dying upset her. Or why the thought of losing my dad, *on her watch*, as she called it, made her crazy.

Trent was with us now, while Mum stayed home with a sleeping Sonny. We hadn't told Sonny about his mum and dad yet. It could wait. Let him have one more night of peaceful sleep, dreaming of Superman.

Anna pulled over. We got out of her car three doors up from the Armstrong house. We were ready. Well, as ready as we could be. I recalled everything Hamish had said to me about Anubis – how I was able to resurrect the dead. I wanted to tell Anna, but it wasn't the time or place. Not just yet.

The clouds hung thick and blackened the night sky. The rain halted, with only its remnants glistening off the road like diamonds. Wind whipped the streets, and the smell of rain was subsumed by the stench of Aidah's house.

'That smell.' Anna screwed up her nose.

'She's not even trying to hide from us now. She's gone full-stink ninja.' I pulled my shirt up over my nose.

'You suppose anyone else can smell it?' Anna said, as she joined me on the pavement.

'I think it's all just for us.'

'Would be silly for me to think this was an ambush, and we had the upper hand, wouldn't it,' Anna said, more like a statement than anything else.

'Yeah,' I said. 'Sorry, but she definitely knows we're on our way.' I turned back to the car. 'You coming, or what?'

Trent opened the back door of the Fiesta. He threw his bag over his shoulder. 'Yeah, I'm coming.' He wiped his nose on his sleeve.

I was hesitant about bringing him, but if we were right about Aidah causing the car crash, then no one deserved to take her out more. I don't think I could have kept him from coming, even if I'd wanted to. And if he'd gone on his own, Sonny really would be alone in the world.

My joints suddenly felt weak.

My vision blurred and I wobbled. *Megan's inside, Mouse.* Someone spoke to me. I didn't know if it was Catalina. There was no music or lilac, but it felt light – like a voice I could trust.

'Are you all right?' Trent and Anna held me up.

I exhaled. 'No. I'm crappy. Like *really* crappy. But I'm pretty sure you're worse, Trent. And this is no time to go soft.'

He nodded. 'What did you see just now?'

'More like what I heard. Megan's inside.'

'Damn it.' Anna stared at the house. 'Damn it!'

'Shhh, it's okay. I know what to do for Megan. I swear, I take back everything bad I said about my visitas, even though they've been coming at some extremely inopportune times. They've given me everything I need to know.'

Anna smiled and nodded. 'Of course, kiddo. We'll do whatever you say. I guess it's time I stopped calling you that, huh?' Anna was looking at me strangely.

'What's that?' I said.

'Never mind. Following you, Modesta.'

'Thanks, Anna.'

'Whoa, do you see this?' Anna whispered, as we neared the house.

Trent stared, mouth agape. 'The house being eaten up by the ground? Yeah, I see it. The weeds look like they're pulling the house to Hell where it belongs.'

'Everything's falling apart,' I whispered.

'Not fast enough,' said Anna.

I ran around the side of the neighbour's property. Anna and Trent followed me over the fence into the Armstrong's yard. We tiptoed around the side.

Hamish was there waiting for us. 'Hurry up and get inside,' he whispered. 'Trent, boost Anna and Mouse, and I'll lift you through.' Trent seemed shocked that Hamish spoke directly to him. He boosted Anna and me through the window all the same, then got a hand-up from Hamish.

Trent brushed off his clothes while Hamish closed the window and curtains.

'Sit,' I gestured for everyone to take a seat on Hamish's bed. The place I'd spent the afternoon. There was an ache in my heart as I looked at him. All three of them complied and took a seat. 'The entity which resides in Aidah's body is called 'Sacmis.' We shall call her this now, out of respect for Hamish's mother, who died a long time ago.

'Sacmis is a water witch. When a witch like Sacmis uses a body, she can drain the agua from others to make that body last. Children are best. They have more energy. Sacmis is very clever, in that she drains a little, and if the child should die, she resurrects it and drains it again.'

Hamish lowered his eyes, ashamed and unable to look at us. I continued. 'When that body is finally exhausted, which can take thousands of years, the water witch moves closer and closer to a large body of water, like the ocean, to ensure her survival. There have been other signs indicating Sacmis' desire to swap bodies. However, for a witch as old as Sacmis, she's not nearly as powerful as she should be. She couldn't even register me as an enemy until late in the game. And when she shows her true self, she's translucent. I saw her in my vision, the day she took your mother's body, Hamish. I could almost see straight through her. Sacmis is becoming like that again now. I thought I could take a pretty good guess who's body she wanted next. However, little Sonny Albright has proven himself to be someone far more important than all of us put together. He cast out a powerful bruja del agua in a matter of seconds. I believe Sacmis is here for him. And we are simply in the way.

Our plan is to lure Sacmis. Trent and I will hold the circle so she doesn't get past to escape.' Hamish nodded. His breath was quickening. 'Our job now,' I said, 'is to get Sacmis at her weakest, and to make sure she doesn't transfer to another body other than mine. You can help us, Hamish, or let us do what needs to be done. But either way, when it is done, you will be free. Make your choice.'

Hamish looked at me. 'You already know my choice.'

'Say it now.'

'I'll help you.'

'Your job is Megan.'

'Whatever you say.'

A while later, Trent, Anna, Hamish, and I said our goodbyes to each other. It was better to say goodbye now, than to never get the chance. Hamish grabbed my arms and pulled me in. He whispered in my ear. 'Thank you.'

'Goodbye, Hamish.'

'Are you ever going to say something else to me?'

'If I said anymore, I'd change my mind about this.'

He nodded. 'Take care, Modesta.' He squeezed my hand and turned away. Trent moved over to me to stop me from looking back.

He held me up. 'You're okay. Think of Sonny now.'

I inhaled deeply. 'Okay. This ends.'

CHAPTER 16

MEGAN SAT ON THE FLOOR in the centre of the lounge room. She was slouched, legs crossed, her hair falling over her face, eyes closed and skin oh-so-pale. She looked so very small.

I had to watch my step. The house was caving in.

The plasterboard on the walls in the living room was full of holes and mould. The dank odour of water-rotted wood nearly made me gag. The house swelled. Drips flowed from the ceiling, and the grass from outside grew up through the cracks, creeping in like thieves in the night. I felt the horrid sick humidity in every cell. Not the good kind, where you dipped your hot body in the ocean, or the rain after a muggy day, but the kind that seeped into your lungs and made you ill. I was afraid to breathe the air.

Megan looked up. Her eyes were vacant. Her little face was covered in a mass of sick sweat and she rocked gently, back and forth. A soft moan escaped her lips.

The floor beneath me creaked. The house shifted. The tiles cracked open.

Sacmis moved in through the living room door and stared at us. Her body was sagging. I wasn't sure why she wasn't lasting if she'd taken the Albrights recently. Maybe it was too little, too late.

'Mum. What's happening to you?' Hamish whispered.

Sacmis' mouth opened into a gaping blackness, her neck stretched, and a guttural laugh escaped. 'You useless kid.' Her voice sounded like there were nine of her. 'You useless little boy!' she shrieked. She cracked her neck, and it looked as if her head would snap right off. 'Helping these wankers! Look at them.' She glared at Anna. 'A stuck-up, abused teacher who thinks she's a witch. Talentless. Hopeless. Alone. Your mother cut you off from your family because you're pathetic. *She* was a real witch. You deserve everything she gave you. Every beating. Every cut and bruise. I'm surprised she didn't drown you at birth like a sack of useless puppies. You should be dead already.'

Anna stood firm. 'Don't let her in,' she said.

Sacmis turned to Trent. 'And this pathetic excuse

for a son. Mummy and Daddy are with me, now, Sunshine. I'll look after them for you.' Sacmis licked her black lips. Trent surged forward and I grabbed his arm.

'No,' I whispered. 'Don't let her get in your head.'

'Modesta.' She glared at me. 'You. YOU! *You* die *today.*'

'You seem annoyed with me, *Sacmis*. Why?' I saw her fists clench.

'You figured out my name. Fiddlydeedee. I'm not Rumplestilskin. Piss off, you little fag hag! That's right. And Trentie pie, does your best friend know you're gay? That you like the little boys?'

Trent raised his eyebrows. 'I like the big boys, *Sunshine*. You're the one who likes them little. You sick, sick woman. Who could love you? Not even your own son.'

I stared at my best friend. He was holding fast.

Sacmis screeched. 'Piss off, dick smoker! I can go back home and eat Sonny Albright for dinner, and Connie Castro for dessert.' She smiled and her teeth were brown and broken, but she wasn't done.

Just like we needed.

Anger fogged the mind. It made you miss important things.

Anna spoke next. 'You have some real Mummy and Daddy issues, don't you? I know what happened to you with your father, Ptah.'

'DON'T YOU SAY HIS NAME!' she came toward us. We held hands.

I pulled the black tourmaline and bloodstones from my pocket and dropped them on the floor before us. 'White light protect us. You shall not cross.' Anna, Hamish and Trent stepped forward, still clutching each other's hands. 'You shall not cross!'

Sacmis stopped in her tracks.

Energy surged through all of us.

Sacmis did what we expected, and turned to Megan, instead. She ran to the girl and pulled her up by the hair. 'You're mine.' She glared at us. 'You've killed her. You've killed her!'

But Megan didn't budge. Sacmis couldn't get her off the ground. She pulled at Megan's hair and it fell out in clumps. She tore at her skin, and the girl came apart like bubble gum stuck to concrete, just like I'd planned. Flaps of slimy skin and protruding bones littered the floor.

'What have you done!?' Sacmis screeched. What was left of Megan melted down into a puddle on the floor.

'Where is she?'

'She's somewhere safe,' I said. 'You're tired, Sacmis. You're losing your edge. We came right in here without your even noticing. You saw exactly what we wanted you to see.'

She laughed. 'Good for you, Little Mouse.' Her demeanour shifted. 'Good for you.' Sacmis walked over to us, calmly now. She looked weak, in fact. If she'd been able to have a taste of Megan, there would've been no stopping her. But *this* Sacmis we might handle.

'Hamish. Darling. Come to Mummy.' Hamish

didn't budge. 'You do as I say.' Sacmis lifted her hand and waved it. Hamish's image flickered like a broken hologram.

'Hamish!' Sacmis screamed. He disappeared completely.

'Betrayed by your only son,' said Anna. 'Your only son. He has Megan safe in his room right now. Neither of them were truly here. A teenage witch just made you see something that wasn't there. She's been practising witchcraft for a mere eight years, Sacmis. *Tssk Tssk.* You should be ashamed of yourself.'

Sacmis poked out that horrible, pointed tongue of hers and came toward me. I could hear the wet, familiar, sucking sound.

'Now, Mouse,' said Trent.

'I invoke the light in my heart,' I said.

Sacmis stopped.

'In the dark, where the evil is, I invoke the light in my heart.'

Sacmis hissed.

'En la oscuridad, donde reside el mal, invoco la luz en mi corazón!'

We raised our hands up high.

Sacmis moved towards us.

'I invoke the spirit of Catalina Castro!' My body rose into the air and I shook. Gold light surrounded me, and the air smelled of fire and burnt wood.

I fell to the floor. As I stood, Sacmis laughed.

'What have you done, Little Mouse? I see nothing here. You disappoint. You silly, silly little girl.

Catalina Castro? Your dead aunty? She's nothing to me. Cat and Mouse? Cat and Mouse? This game is old.' Sacmis rushed forward.

The stones and protective walls no longer worked, and she grabbed my arm and dug her nails in again. Nothing had happened! Trent and Anna seemed frozen.

I'm wanted. Dead or alive.

The tongue. The tongue came out of her mouth and darted toward me. The slithering in my ear, wet and cold. A burning sensation ran through my body.

I was burning!

My plan hadn't worked.

Sacmis drew and pulled.

'*Sirenita,*' said Cat in my ear. 'I'm here. I'm ready.' I exhaled. She was here. It was going to be okay. 'Watch how it's done, little mermaid.'

Cat's soul was wrenched right out of me and into Sacmis' body.

Sacmis stopped – her eyes large and her mouth agape. 'What… what…'

'What's the matter?' I said, smiling. 'Cat got your tongue?'

There was a sizzling sound followed by a piercing whistle. 'Get back!' I called. The sound of a giant kettle boiling on the stove filled the room as the three of us moved away. We barrelled around the doorways and flung ourselves into the hall.

Sacmis shrieked. An ear-splitting explosion followed. I could hear water splatter onto the walls.

I imagined blood and pieces of flesh flying about the room. A fizzling sound could be heard, and then steam surrounded me as I lay on the tiles.

Then there was silence. I waited.

I don't know how long I waited, but I didn't want to get up off that hallway floor for fear of what I'd find. I couldn't bear to see Anna or Trent hurt. Were they beside me? Or maybe even Sacmis was inside one of them somehow. I wanted to stay here on the white tiles with my eyes closed and my false sense of security intact.

I forced myself up, anyway.

The ankh around my neck were so heavy. The chains felt like they were cutting into my neck. I took them off and placed them on the floor beside me.

They disappeared.

Trent and Anna were huddled in the hall, both breathing, thank the Gods. Aidah's body, no longer controlled by Sacmis, was heaped on the floor like a skeleton waiting to be displayed in biology class. There were no pieces of her painting the walls.

I bent down to touch Aidah. She fell to ashes in a pile on the floor.

'Mouse?' Cat was speaking to me. 'Mouse.' Her voice wasn't in my head, it was coming from behind me. I turned to see her, standing right there, as if flesh and bone. I ran to embrace her.

'I've not got long, *Sirenita*. Trent and Anna are fine. Look after them both. I'll look after Hamish. His soul is a long time coming.' Cat smiled.

I held her. 'I love you, Cat. I miss you so much.'

'I love you, too. And I'm proud of you, Modesta. Don't be afraid of the gift you have. Sonny is special. But together, you will be unstoppable. Listen now. You must go into Sacmis' room, and open her wooden chest. You have the key.'

I looked into my palm. There was a key there. 'What's it…' When I looked up, she was gone. 'You always were pretty terrible at saying goodbye before you hung up the phone.'

Trent and Anna got up.

'It's almost over,' I said. 'Go to Hamish's room. Megan will be scared. Hamish has likely … he's gone, and she'll be afraid.' Trent and Anna dashed off down the hall.

I found the master bedroom again easily enough. On the surface, it was like the bedroom of a mother who shopped at thrift stores, not a woman who was possessed for centuries by a demon. We'd found nothing the last time, but this time a chest sat by the end of the bed. It was engraved with *Enteroctopus dofleini*. A North Pacific giant octopus looked at me from the engraved ocean as I turned the key and opened the mysterious box. Inside was a black bag, and as I lifted it, I heard metal clinking. I peered inside. Black metal greeted my inquiring eyes. There were hundreds of ankh, all shapes and sizes and made from all sorts of materials jumbled together in the bag. Before I could reach in, I was startled by laughter. Wind whistled in and opened the window shutters.

It danced around me, lifting my hair. I smelled the ocean. The laughter grew louder, and the bag in my hand opened wider. A light poured out of it. Gold, white, turquoise, jade, amber, and crimson swirled out and filled the air above me.

'Thank you,' someone whispered, and there were chuckles. More voices echoed, *thank you,* and I could hear all of them both individually and as a harmonised group at the same time. Cool fingers caressed my shoulders and I shivered.

I waited for Hamish, but he didn't come. I supposed he'd already gone, as I remembered Cat's words, *his soul is a long time coming.* I wondered how he felt now – the relief of sweet release at last.

It was a long time before the lights went away, and after they did, I was left standing there with nothing more exotic than a bag of jewellery in an empty, normal house.

I ran to Hamish's room. He had disappeared. Anna was holding onto a tearful Megan.

'They're free,' I breathed. Trent hugged me.

Anna nodded in understanding. 'You did it.'

'Hamish is gone.' My stomach tightened.

'I'm sorry you didn't get to be friends,' said Anna.

'He was … exceptional.' I studied my fingers. 'An exceptional person with everything he'd been through. I wouldn't have lasted.'

'I believe you would have, Mouse. But yes, despite everything, his kindness prevailed,' said Anna.

Trent's hair was all over the place, and he looked

like he'd been out all night partying. 'Well, I feel like I've been hit by a truck that then backed up and hit me again.'

I put an arm around his shoulder. 'I'm sorry about your parents,' I whispered. 'We were so focussed on protecting Sonny.'

Trent nodded. 'We can talk about it later. Right now, we need to get Megan home. Again.'

Mum, Trent, Anna, and I sat on the grass looking out to the ocean at Burleigh Headland. Sonny laughed and ran around with Bruno, who snorted, huffed, and drooled on him. Sonny had cried most of the morning, but a child can only mourn on and off, and the dog was good for taking his mind off things. It was terrible to think of Sonny growing up without Rick and Carey, especially with his *abilities*. The entire Gold Coast would feel the loss. Nanna Albright was devastated.

'I'll keep running the vans this week until I can find someone to take over,' said Trent.

'I'll go with you,' I said.

'We'll all pitch in,' said Anna.

'You and Sonny will stay with Nanna Albright?' Mum asked Trent.

'Yes,' he smiled. 'And Bruno.'

The wind was fresh and cool. Megan was home

now with her parents, with little memory as to what happened, thanks to Anna. Her parents were confused as to why she kept 'running away,' but it was best they never know the alternative.

Trent stood and went to join Sonny and Bruno on the grass.

'Hamish is finally free, Mouse. You did that for him,' said Anna.

'It was something he couldn't do for himself, Modesta,' Mum said. 'You set free his true mother, as well. They'll be together as we speak. Remember them like that, and you soon see the silver lining.'

'Thanks, Mum. That helps. I would assume you do that with Cat?' I asked.

Anna looked up at us. Mum nodded. '*Sí*. It helps to think that way.'

'I might need you to remind me every now and then.'

'That, I can do.' Mum put her arm around my shoulders. 'I knows you do not believe this, Modesta. But God has a plan. You are sometimes asked to intervene. Sometimes you are not. Sometimes, people must go to him, and there's nothing you can do about it.'

'You really believe that, don't you, Mum?'

She squeezed my hand. 'I do, my angel. Most the definitely ... I do.'

ABOUT THE AUTHOR

Hayley Merelle Clearihan (HMC) is a freelance writer, teacher, and artist who resides on the Gold Coast, Australia. She has a degree in psychology, writes a column for an online magazine, and blogs about global issues like the beauty myth, asylum seekers, and gay rights. Hayley also believes in magic.

See her official site here:
www.HMCWriter.com

Join her on Facebook:
www.facebook.com/hmcwriter

Join her on Twitter:
www.twitter.com/hmcwrite

Made in the USA
Charleston, SC
16 October 2015